CHRISTOPHER BURNS

Christopher Burns was born in 1944 in the small town of Egremont in Cumbria. He has had three novels published: SNAKEWRIST, THE FLINT BED (which was short-listed for the Whitbread Novel of the Year award in 1989), and THE CONDITION OF ICE. His stories have appeared in the *London Review of Books*, *London Magazine* and the *Critical Quarterly*. He was also featured in Heinemann's *Best Short Stories* in 1986 and 1988. He is married with two sons and lives in Cumbria.

Christopher Burns

ABOUT THE BODY

First published in Great Britain in 1988 by Martin Secker & Warburg Ltd.

Sceptre edition, 1990

Sceptre is an imprint of Hodder and Stoughton Paperbacks, a division of Hodder and Stoughton Ltd.

British Library C.I.P.

Burns, Christopher, *1944*–
  About the body.
  I. Title
  823'.914 [F]

ISBN 0-340-52564-9

Printed and bound in Great Britain for Hodder and Stoughton Paperbacks, a division of Hodder and Stoughton Ltd., Mill Road, Dunton Green, Sevenoaks, Kent TN13 2YA. (Editorial Office: 47 Bedford Square, London WC1B 3DP) by Richard Clay Ltd., Bungay, Suffolk.

For my mother and father

CONTENTS

EMBRACING THE SLAUGHTERER

THERE ARE only two of us in the house. Neither knows the other's name. We have been here for three weeks.

The house is pleasant, although some of the white paint has begun to turn yellow and there are hairline cracks in the plaster. We each have our own small bedroom but, since there are only two rooms downstairs, I often sit in the kitchen at night reading at the table while my companion watches television or plays his video games on it. The house lies in a quiet, slightly dilapidated cul-de-sac and has, at the rear, a small garden enclosed by high brick walls. At its far end is a shelter and, beyond the boundary wall, an access road giving on to the levelled site of an old warehouse. From the back bedroom, the one that the other man occupies, you can see beyond it to the river. Further downstream the dockyard cranes are clustered.

Every morning, at the same time, the telephone rings. It stands on a small table at the bottom of the stairs, but there are no directories beneath it because they have all been taken away. I answer. The call is always short, often no more than a few seconds. The other man stands in the kitchen, waiting. I make sure I do not look at him while I answer.

When I replace the receiver and turn to him he looks very young, his features almost transparent. 'Not today?' he asks.

'No, not today.'

This has happened since our first day here, and will happen until our last.

He is a thin-faced boy, with high cheekbones and a wispy beard which he strokes and pulls, apparently absent-mindedly, as if constant stimulation would thicken it. He has blue eyes which can appear quite startling at times; he could have learned to make more use of them, I think. And I can tell that he finds my attitudes, even my dress sense, puzzling and perhaps inappropriate. I have never worn jeans; he lives in his as if he has never worn anything else. Once, while I was ironing one of my shirts, he asked if I owned more than two suits. I answered him truthfully, adding that I also had a dinner jacket. I knew that he would see this as a betrayal, and before he could speak I added that I had no qualms about wearing it, and no guilt either. He asked me if I ever worried about appearing to be on the wrong side. I gave him my best saturnine smile, and explained that I was on the side, not of a particular style, but of justice.

He nodded. I could see him turning this over in his head. He had a dullish but malleable mind. Buttressed by a few quotations and slogans, he can rationalise whatever he wants. This, and his energy, would have made him valuable, and his confidence would have been increased by some minor operations – a post office raid, perhaps, or the killing of one of the softer targets. I do not know what has brought him to this house, and I do not wish to know.

He has adjusted to my presence and his uncertainty and nervousness have at last begun to quieten. As if to prove himself, he still quotes from the approved sources. I noticed very early, however, that he has scant knowledge of any body of work or thought, and that all he needs to keep him going are these nuggets, produced with the flair of holy writ.

This morning it is St-Just; yesterday it was Machiavelli. No doubt he thinks of himself as very international. He had not, however, heard of the dictum on the necessity of killing the sons of Brutus, although he pretended he had.

'Personally,' I say, quite slowly, 'I find that Brecht has a lot to say on all these matters.'

'Oh yes?' he asks, cautiously.

I quote from *Die Massnahme*:

> Sink in the dirt,
> Embrace the slaughterer,
> But change the world; the world needs it.

He still seems very suspicious.

'It was the favourite reading of the Baader-Meinhof group,' I explain. 'I can say it in the original German if you want.'

His face becomes momentarily flushed with emotion. 'Yes, I'm sure you can. Why do you try to be so superior to me? Is that part of the preparations, as well?'

'I shall not pretend to be that which I am not. I have lived a different kind of life to you.'

'What's your name, then? If we are to have honesty, at least tell me your name.'

'You know that that is impossible. It makes things easier if neither of us knows the other's name.'

'I'll tell you mine. You can't stop me.'

'If you do, I shall not hear it. Believe me. I have a lot of experience in these things.'

Suddenly he is deflated. 'That's the ruling,' he says quietly, as if all the anger has fled.

'And we should not query it. We are here to make sure the orders are carried out.'

'Both of us?'

'We each have been given a part. I know you won't let me down.'

'And you?'

'You know that I'm an expert. Nothing will go amiss.'

I have hidden nothing from him. The pistol, with its screw-on silencer, is kept in a drawer in my bedroom. He can get it if he wants, although I keep the clip. A week or so ago I found him examining the gun. He handled it carefully, almost reverentially, until in a quick flurry of bravado he whirled it round his finger and took a sighting down the barrel. The mood passed and he replaced it as carefully as an ornithologist replaces the egg of a rare bird. When he looked up at me, his smile was half in embarrassment, half in challenge.

I have often taken him, at his request, to the bottom of the garden. Today we do the same. The garden is full of the yellow heads of dandelions and, just before the shelter, a patch of tall nettles has fallen across the path. We have to walk round the nettles to get to the shelter.

He stands on the flagstones, out of the sun, looking round as if he expects to see something new. Nothing has changed. The corrugated roof has smears of rust around the bolts; the door to the back street is still barred, although I have treated the hinges and padlock with some oil. He notices this, but I shake my head to show that there is nothing significant.

'And afterwards,' he asks, 'the car? The river?'

I nod. It helps settle a man if there is no mystery. He appears satisfied.

On the way back, he asks 'How many –' then he stops, unsure of the next word.

'Operations,' I suggest.

He accepts it. '– have you done?'

'Seven or eight.'

'You're not sure?'

'This is the eighth.'

There is a short pause, then a decisive question. 'Does that include the ones that were called off?'

'No.'

'How many were they?'

'Not many.'

'Aren't you allowed to give me a figure?'

'Two.'

'The odds could be worse,' he says after a while, as I lock the house door behind us. 'You were disappointed when they were called off? Pleased? Relieved?'

'They were operations, nothing more. I got paid anyway.'

'I don't believe you.'

'As you wish.'

He goes into the living-room and turns on the television. I sigh. I am growing tired of the things he finds so soothing. I have given up trying to teach him chess. Even though he understood that the game would be perfect for passing time, he had little aptitude and showed no real interest. He operates on a much more emotional level.

I sit at the kitchen table and put on my headphones. Bach.

'Are you hungry?' I ask him half an hour later.

'Yes, yes I am.'

'What would you like?'

The freezer has been filled with easily cooked dishes, and I am becoming bored. I have already eaten the better meals, and even persuaded my companion to try them. I was astonished at how unimaginative his tastes were. He accused me of being an élitist; a poor argument, especially from one who never rose higher than junk food. Good food and wine, I told him, should not be the province of the merely wealthy, just as high culture must, if it is to survive, be taken up once more by the masses.

This time he comes through into the kitchen and searches through the packets. 'They're getting down. There are only a couple of days left.' He looks up at me accusingly.

'I'll order some more; it presents no real difficulty.'

'Is that usual?'

'I was at a house once where we waited for six months. We had to restock several times.'

'And at the end of six months?'

'Policy had changed.'

'That was one of your two special cases, was it?'

'My partn. rose in the ranks after that. So you see, anything is possible.'

'Who was he?'

'You know I won't tell you that.'

'You would tell no one?'

'Of course not.'

'Then you must represent a danger to him. He must resent you, surely. Be plotting against you.'

'Possibly. But, at this particular moment, all I am concerned about is our meal.'

He makes an odd, almost effeminate movement with his hand. 'Whatever you think.'

I have thought it all out beforehand, but I pretend to be thinking of it just at this moment when I say 'I shall make you a Basque dish, a *pipérade*.' I find his suspicious frown amusing, but I keep my own face straight. 'It's all right, it's basically a peasant dish, so for you at least it will be ideologically sound. I shall make it as a vegetable *purée* thickened with eggs. Will you like that, do you think?'

'I don't know. I don't speak French.'

'I'm sure you'll like it. I spent some time with our Basque friends a few years ago, so I know a little about their food. It was an exchange, you understand; we discussed techniques, strategy – it was all very useful. Of course, there *is* a problem.'

'Go on.'

'I need to buy the ingredients. We have onions and eggs here, but no peppers or garlic. And I prefer to select the tomatoes myself. If I can get French or Spanish ones, or even Italians, so much the better.'

'You can leave me here. I won't do anything stupid. I give you my word on that.'

I nod. 'I appreciate that. But perhaps you would prefer another way. You could come with me. I need another pair of hands. The pistol goes in the shoulderholster, just in case we're spotted.'

'You'd let me do that? You don't think it's too risky?'

'Behave yourself and there will be no problems. I can trust you – yes?'

He nods with the eagerness of a child promising to be good.

So we walk to the end of the next street, stand at a bus stop for a few minutes behind two Jamaicans, and then take the short ride to the market. I take him round the stalls, telling him how to judge vegetables and fruit and, on the way, buying all we need for the *pipérade*. The openness and freedom mesmerise him. I even let him walk round the clothes stalls, where he looks at a James Dean teeshirt as if he is thinking of buying it. I remind him that he does not have any money; it would be cruel to say, at this moment, that there is no point. Nevertheless he looks hurt when, at a secondhand bookstall, I spot an out-of-print Pasolini translation and pay a pound for it.

The sky turns grey and a persistent drizzle begins to sweep across the city. Our last call is at a wine shop, although they do not have any Jurançon so I settle for a cheap Roussillon white. We have to huddle together in a doorway while waiting for the return bus.

Back in the flat he is relaxed, and apparently content. While I busy myself with the meal he sits in the kitchen, his chair tilted so that he can seesaw on the back legs. He reminisces about a childhood holiday spent beside a river, with willows on the bank that brushed the water, and owls that hunted the meadows at dusk, and the constant slow heavy presence of cattle.

At last I can serve the food and sit opposite him. 'Eat up,' I say, 'I guarantee you'll enjoy it.'

He is not sure at first, but after a few mouthfuls he begins to eat more heartily. 'Good?' I ask him, and he nods. He cannot have expected to like it.

'A bit heavy on the garlic,' he says after a while.

'I cut down on the amount just for you.'

'Oh. Is it too mild, then?'

'Not at all. It's just that, if there had only been me, I would have put more in. Have some wine.'

He sips it. 'I'm not sure about this.'

Neither am I, but for different reasons. 'It's all right for the price, I suppose.'

He takes another drink, too long a one, and looks at me. 'Strange this, isn't it. You and I enjoying a meal together.'

'Not too strange. Men have need of companionship. Of whatever kind.'

'I didn't think it would be like this.'

'It always is. Each of us colludes with the forces that shape our ends. It is better that way; one must accept that.'

He picks up the wine bottle and squints at it. 'Enough for another couple. Want another?'

I nod and he fills both our glasses, although he is not so competent as to prevent a little from spilling on the tablecloth.

When he puts down the bottle, I see a drop race from the neck to the shoulder, then slow down as if it will poise on the glass, finally to trickle on to the tablemat on which the bottle rests. I lift my glass and the telephone rings.

It has never rung at this time before. He looks startled and fearful. 'A wrong number?' he asks.

'Perhaps.' I do not make the mistake of letting him see my face as I answer. And, when I hang up, I try to let my expression remain unaltered, although I can feel a tightening of the facial muscles.

He knows. His own face betrays it. He tries to say something, but cannot.

I nod calmly. 'This is it.'

At first it appears that he cannot respond, but then he asks, with an odd inflexion as if attempting nonchalance, 'Tomorrow?'

'They say there can be no delay.'

He shakes himself, then stands up. The chairleg squeals on the kitchen floor. He is as straight as a child playing at parades. I go for the pistol and walk back towards him at an even, unflappable pace. His eyes are on me as I fix the silencer; they are as wide as if he stood in the dark.

'Straight away,' I say.

'I have to –' he says, then breaks off as if sudden embarrassment has seized him.

'All right, but the car is already on its way.'

He closes the lavatory door but I cannot hear him bolt it. I stand outside with the pistol at my side. Soon I can hear the cistern flush and fill, and the noise of water swishing in the basin as he washes his hands. He comes out. His face is pale. 'Let's get it over with,' he says.

I walk with him to the back door and unlock it. We walk out into the garden. The rain has stopped and, apart from a few massive grey clouds, still edged with sunlight, the sky is awash with a darkening blue. He holds his arms tightly around himself, possibly to stop them from trembling.

He turns to me. 'You'll tell them how I took it?'

I indicate he should go down the path. 'There's no time to lose. We each have our orders.'

'Please.'

'Yes, I promise I'll tell them. When the phone next rings, I'll tell them.'

He sets off down the garden. I follow him, one step behind. He walks with a kind of pride, but jerkily, as if he has been wounded. He goes towards his fate content, because he no longer thinks he can avoid it. We all collaborate, even with our own destruction.

The nettles block our path. In the evening shadow they look grey. We step around them and walk under the shelter. Beneath the roof everything is dark and the rain has brought out the smells of earth, moss and damp mortar. I am eager to have everything finished now.

'Kneel down,' I say. There is no time for last words; I know that I will not wish to make them.

Without a word he obeys, kneeling on the flagstones with his hands clasped together as if in prayer. I wait for a few seconds while my eyes adjust to the dark; when my time comes, I will not want my companion to be less than precise.

I angle the pistol carefully, not wishing to startle him by letting the metal touch the back of his neck.

JOHN'S RETURN TO LIVERPOOL

HE CAME to the door during the first frost of winter. Straight away she knew who he was.

'You've come back,' she said.

In the streetlight he looked bloodless. Behind him frost began to settle on the grass and blind the windows of parked cars. Children in heavy boots careered between the houses, turned corners sharply, yelled to each other through the drifting cold.

His hair was damp and his nose was thinner than it should have been. She thought of how she'd read that sniffing cocaine destroys the bridges, then felt guilty that such a small thing should have crossed her mind. It was nothing compared to the magnitude of his return.

His skin was waxen, as if it had been newly laid across the bones. 'Can I come in?' he asked simply.

She didn't feel she had to say anything.

He sat down beside the coal fire but kept on his thick blue coat. Its shoulders sparkled with frost. His glasses misted up with the temperature change and he unhooked them from his ears, cleaning them absent-mindedly with a handkerchief. They were the familiar round frames. She noticed his hands were thinner and bonier than she remembered or expected.

'You've lost a lot of weight,' she said quietly.

He nodded.

Dorothy got down on her knees in front of him and looked straight into his eyes. Without the glasses they looked short-sighted and introspective. 'The pounds have dropped off you,' she said, 'you can tell just by looking at you. Your face is a lot thinner than it was. You were quite beefy when I knew you.

There are lines under your eyes and your nose is so thin it looks like a blade.'

'I was too fat a lot of the time in the early days.' Despite all the years his voice was still flat and nasal.

'That may be, but now you're much too thin. I used to think that, you know. All that macrobiotic food isn't for you.'

He smiled.

'John, you need a good feed.'

He shook his head. 'No. No food. I can't. But I still need sleep.'

'Are you tired now?'

'I get tired very quickly. It's as if everything has drained away. All those energy levels just aren't there anymore.'

'They'll come back,' she said comfortingly. The firelight danced in his eyes. 'You can have the spare bed. But first you must have a hot bath. The fire's been on all day so there's plenty of hot water. Don't argue, you need to get the cold out of your bones. It's been a long time, John.'

'More than twenty years.'

'I'm pleased you remembered me. Honoured.'

'I was never any good at keeping in touch. You know that.'

'A lot happened. I got married.' He looked suddenly uncertain, and she laughed. 'Don't worry, it finished long ago. All I have left of him are a few photographs, some of his clothes and an old wedding certificate.' Suddenly she felt tears at the corners of her eyes. They were so sharp they stung her and she shook her head in disbelief. 'I still can't believe it's you.'

'Oh, it's me all right. No doubt about it. Flesh and blood.' He extended his hands and she grasped them, feeling the skin and the bones. She moved her fingers round until she could feel the slow pulse in his wrists.

She couldn't hold back the tears. They slid down her face. 'You knew that if you ever wanted me I'd be here.'

He nodded slowly, as if preoccupied.

She sniffed (she thought it sounded horrible) and said firmly '*Bath*.'

'All right. Whatever you say. If I can stay . . .'

'Of *course* you're staying. For as long as you want. Now, come on. You look as if you haven't been warm for days and your hair's in bad need of a wash.'

At that moment his eyes looked uncomprehending.

'I'm not giving you a choice, John.'

'Okay.'

She ran the bath until the room was full of steam and dappled glass. He stood and let her undress him, making no protest, as silent as a patient. In the bath his feet stuck out of the water and she placed them on either side of the chrome taps. She washed his hair several times, relathering it, feeling it become cleaner beneath her fingers. She left him soaking while she washed his clothes. They had expensive labels but felt as if he'd been sleeping rough in them. She left the bathroom door open in case, in a trance with the heat, he slipped beneath the water.

When she dried him he felt warmer, healthier, more human. The water that dripped from his hair was warm. He even began to smile. He stood there, still pale but a little more pink, while she rubbed him dry with a thick white towel. She felt the ribs, the muscle wall, the relaxed skin of his genitals, the slow thump of the heart. It was then that she asked him about the marks. They were distinct pinkish circles, almost like immature nipples.

'What are these?' she asked, trying not to sound as nervous as she felt.

He looked down.

'You must know,' he said.

'Are they where the bullets hit?'

He nodded.

She tried to be calm, as calm as she could. 'John,' she asked, 'are you dead?'

He laughed. He pushed his hair back with one hand. 'Of course I'm dead,' he said, 'can't you tell? Don't you believe what you read in the papers?'

Later John sat in her husband's dressing gown in front of the fire. He stared into its flames, watching the black coal burning. He seemed content.

When he slept his hair fell across his eyes in a fine swathe, making him look almost boyish. She pushed it gently back from his eyelids with her fingertips. He drew the blankets tightly about him like a child.

That night while he slept Dorothy filled his room with mementos of his life – posters, records, fan magazines, old photographs, a couple of books, a guitar with his name scrawled across it. Then she lay in bed, with a warm tide of fulfilment and trust flowing through her. She stayed awake like a guardian, and thought of him waking like a child at Christmas, lost in wonder at the Aladdin's cave of his own past.

He was already awake when she looked in. He sat by the bed in her husband's broadly striped pyjamas. He picked through the collection, never dwelling for long on anything, but sometimes smiling and sometimes looking puzzled at this accumulation of evidence. Later she brought out the photograph album and together they looked at the pictures.

'You must have been our first fan,' John said.

'I never claimed that.'

'Didn't you? But you were always there. I remember we all liked to see you. You gave us a sense of security.'

'I remember I felt quite possessive about you. When you started to make it big I thought you were being stolen by others. Firstly girls from Liverpool, then Hamburg, London –'

'Tomorrow the world,' he said, and the cutting edge was in his voice. 'Where was this taken?'

'Don't you recognise Matthew Street?'

'Christ. Yes.'

'Do you know everyone on it?'

'That's me. And you, and that girl who used to sometimes come with you. With Pete Best, George. That's Ringo when he was with Rory Storm. That's Rory's girlfriend. This must have been just after Stu died.'

'Not long. We were all terribly upset about that.'

He put his hand up to his face and spread his fingers in an unexpectedly feminine motion.

'We wanted Paul on the photo but it all got a bit chaotic,'

she laughed. 'He came back to line up the camera with me and I took this by mistake. I just pressed the shutter too soon. And it was the end of the film.'

He tilted his head back and laughed. She could see hollows at the base of his neck. 'Look,' he said, 'I can remember a lot about those days. All of a sudden.'

They reminisced about the old days. About old songs, places, friends. Endless loves that had lasted a few days, wild ambitions that were never airborne; a time when all the future had lain itself before them. John was relaxed and amusing, telling tall stories, most of them true, with all his old flair for pithiness and zest.

'Come on,' she said finally, 'it's time you ate.'

He shook his head.

'It's more than twelve hours since you arrived,' she said, 'and you haven't eaten or drunk a thing. You must *try*.'

'No,' he said, 'leave it.'

She left it a moment and then said, 'It'll do you good to have a meal.'

'Don't let me stop you,' he said.

So she ate on her own.

Later she dressed him in a pair of jeans and a black sweater. They were both slightly too big for him. 'His shoes will be a size too large, as well,' she mused. 'Maybe we could find some really thick socks so they won't be too uncomfortable.'

'You know, I'll have to revisit the old places.'

She nodded. 'I knew they could never kill you,' she said. 'I knew you'd come back.'

He thought about this for a long time. 'I always knew it was possible,' he said at last. 'We thought about it a lot.'

'What happened? What *really* happened?'

'He got me all right. You go through life tensed up for the unexpected, and when it happens . . .'

He gripped her by the arm. She felt her limb go numb the grip was so tight.

'You mustn't tell anyone,' he said. There was urgency and a slight bitterness in his voice.

She shook her head, mute.

'I mean it,' he said, and all the old menace and unpredictability were there. 'No one must ever know.'

'I swear it.'

'No one.'

'My arm hurts.'

He let go of her. 'Sorry,' he said.

Within a few days he was leaving her for several hours, slipping out of the house at dusk with a turned-up coat collar and a pulled-down hat. Sometimes when he returned he would tell her where he had been – to where his mother lived, or Aunt Mimi's old house, or Penny Lane, or Matthew Street, or Strawberry Fields. Sometimes he said nothing, but stared into the fire, red light edging his face. She would pretend to watch the television but all the time keep her eyes on him. He still had not eaten, and she was becoming increasingly concerned. She once suggested calling a doctor and he was mercilessly sarcastic to her, asking did she not know that a doctor could do nothing for the dead – only angels and undertakers were of any use to the dead.

So she prepared rich, hot, heavy-smelling meals for herself, hoping that they would somehow trigger hunger in him. But he remained indifferent, and all the time got thinner.

And although at times he was his old charming self, he often drifted away into silence and introspection, gazing for long periods at nothing. In this relaxed, almost exhausted posture he looked like a man recuperating, lost between ordeals, resting between battles. It was then that he became a stranger, a foreigner in his own land, unwilling or unable to grasp the everyday event. He had no trouble in refusing to answer her.

Over the next few days he offered her four versions of the afterlife. She only asked him about it once but he could not let the matter rest. When he described them there was an edge to his voice. He was like a man betrayed, cheated out of his inheritance.

In the first of these he told her of an afterlife like a children's heaven. There he would meet again all those he had loved, including the famous Julia, his mother. 'She's there all right,' he said, eyes glittering, 'it's just the way you think it should be. All your friends, all your relations. It's like one big, endless, happy childhood. Like soft, neverending protection. The lion lies down with the lamb.'

The second was a rock'n'roll heaven. 'They're all up there,' he said, moving his hand in a slow arc and looking up at the ceiling. He was like a parody preacher. 'Presley, Hendrix, Holly. They make music too great for mortal ears. And the girls are always beautiful and always available.' He stared directly at her, daring her to take him seriously.

A third version, the Eastern version, spoke of cycles of incarnation, of moments of insight between death and birth during which one saw with a clarity that Earth could never match. Life was an ascent or descent through stages of self-knowledge. One plunged down the spiral towards the senseless and inanimate or crawled up it towards the angels.

'And you?' Dorothy asked.

He sneered. 'Why,' he said, 'I've always known where I was going. To the toppermost of the poppermost.' It was the half-dismissive, half-serious phrase he'd used to cajole and encourage the others when they'd been struggling in Hamburg and Liverpool.

But John also offered the possibility of a fourth kind of afterlife. This was a spiritual existence, the survival of the mind without the body in a nexus of consciousness. Identities were individual and yet inseparable from the connection which passed through them. They were pulses in the eternal mind.

'And you've been part of this?'

Suddenly, without warning, he looked stricken and fearful. 'I don't know,' he whispered. She put her arms round him and he buried his head in her bosom. After a few minutes he had recovered.

Of course, she speculated about a fifth version. The dead returned to their old homes, haunting them, were restless and unsatisfied spirits until something finally laid them to rest. But he always felt so real in her arms.

'Come on,' she said to him, 'you're all right, John. You're here with me. You're *safe*.'

'Do you think so?'

'Of course. I know so.'

'None of it's true, Dorothy.'

'What? What isn't?'

His eyes were startling and honest, his cheeks thin. His hands looked large on the end of stick-like arms. 'It's oblivion, you know,' he said, matter-of-fact. 'Everything just sputters to an end, the body systems close down, consciousness just folds in on itself. There's no light, no dark, nothing. It's oblivion. Nothing. For ever.'

She shook her head.

'A dying man's life comes to him in the few moments before the end,' he said bitterly. 'And that's it. You go into death fooling yourself. Our only talent is self-deception.'

That night Dorothy sat and watched television. John was already asleep; his periods of rest were getting longer and longer. Now it was common for him to sleep the clock round. Sometimes when the winter sun set she would ask him if he was going out; he'd shake his head and say he was tired.

She sat with a coffee and watched a soap opera, the news, and a documentary about medicine. In the documentary a doctor discussed the nature of the self. One's feelings were located in the self, he said, and that was paradoxical, for the self was un-locatable. Nobody knew where it was. As an illustration he showed amputees who still experienced sensations in limbs that were no longer there. When something vital is removed, the doctor said, the self creates an alternative – and it is too simple to say that this creation is fictitious. To the self, it is real.

'You've hardly changed at all,' he said to her the next day.

'Haven't I?' She was flattered but surprised.

'You're just like you were all those years ago.' He seemed bemused by this.

She laughed. 'It's nice of you to say so, but it's not really true.'

'It is. You even have the same figure. Girlish – that's the word. People change over the years. Look at me. But you, you're no different. You look twenty-five years younger than me. Why, you even wear the same kind of clothes as you did then.'

'I *don't*.'

He nodded. It was slow. 'You'd think you were still there, Dorothy. All around me it still belongs to the early sixties. There's only me that's different.'

He shuddered. It was a spasm that ran through him, and he hugged his arms to himself to control it.

'I'm outside the time capsule,' he said.

Dorothy stood up and looked at herself in the mirror. Afternoon light made her face white. She bent close to the glass. There were broadening strands of grey in her hair, webbings of lines at her eyes and mouth, and she knew if she pulled down the collar of her blouse she would find the beginnings of a scrawniness at the base of her neck.

John's fingers traced his chest until they found, beneath his clothes, the site of one of the bullets. He spread his hands over the area, pushed the flesh together. He was like a young girl discovering the beginnings of a breast.

'Dorothy.'

'Yes?'

'I'm dying. I know it.'

'You're not, you're *not*.'

'I know it. I've been thinking stupid things, thinking that I'd survived it. I thought that somehow this was all true, that it was real, that I had been given some kind of guarantee.' He tilted his head downward. His hair fell forward. When he spoke again his voice was strained and unstable. 'Because I can reach out and touch things, because I can touch you, I thought that was proof.' He put his hands up to his face.

'John?'

When he looked up again the lower rims of his glasses had caught tears. They spilled out of the sides as he lifted his head. His voice shook. 'It scares me,' he said, 'I'm terrified.'

Once more she had to comfort him. She could feel his bones beneath the skin. There was so little flesh on him now she felt as if she were comforting a famine victim.

'I'm tired,' he whispered.

Even though it was only mid-afternoon she decided to put him to bed. He looked drained and ill, and she had to steady him as he walked to the bedroom. She helped him undress. He insisted that he did not have the strength to get into any pyjamas so she humoured him and let him get into bed naked.

He lay and cried while she sat beside him and held his hand and dried his eyes. Eventually the grief seemed to exhaust him, and he quietened and then slipped into unconsciousness. She sat with him for a while. He still sniffed and trembled in his sleep, but gradually, as he sank deeper, the distress left him.

Dorothy went back to the mirror, took off her clothes and stood in front of it. For several minutes she studied herself, and saw that the light was cruel to her. There was no mistaking her age.

As she stared a feeling of unreality swept through her, loosening her understanding, releasing her grip. She felt floating, unresolved, half-imagined. It was a sickeningly dreamlike sensation, as if she belonged to something or someone else. Weakened, she went back to the bedroom.

John lay beneath the sheets. He was quiet, still; his arms were down by his side and his eyes were closed.

She lifted the sheets and slipped into bed beside him. He was cold. She wrapped herself around him, hoping that the heat of her body would warm him. He hardly moved. She could feel the slow pulse of his heart, the shallow peace of his light breathing.

Her fingers searched until they touched the small round mark of a bullet. She ran her fingertips round it, touching it lightly, gently. After a while, like a newborn animal searching for its mother's teat, she burrowed beneath the blankets, found the wound with her mouth, and fastened her lips around it. Then she lay quietly, waiting for the night.

HOW THINGS ARE PUT TOGETHER

(1)

'WHAT ARE we about to experience?'

Neville looked around the theatre.

'An arrangement of images. A montage.'

Winter light, tentative and without contrast, creeps through the tall windows. Inside the theatre all the electric lights have been switched on, and he can see fragments of them reflected in the lenses of those students who wear glasses. Some sit with pencil ends resting between their lips, or poised above notepads. Someone scratches furiously with a ballpoint that won't work.

Neville waits until the scratching stops, then continues. 'Some of you will already be expecting this example. Many of you will have read ahead. Forget your expectations – just watch the evidence; study the arrangement; think about it.'

They are all looking back at him. Neville is in his late thirties, still has the trace of an accent that can be loosely classed as Northern English, and wears the kind of clothes which are worn by academics ten years younger than he is. His collected essays were remaindered last year but the local bookshop still has its stock on sale at the full price. He nods up at the projectionist. The machine begins to whirr.

Neville walks to the windows. 'Watch,' he says.

The wooden floor creaks a little. Outside the sky is low and heavy, an unreal grey. At this time of year, in such a light, the buildings look flat, like something constructed merely to amuse, a stage set perhaps. Neville can see himself in the glass and, rising behind, the students in their rows. He turns the control that operates the vertical slats of blind and they close together.

The projectionist switches off the lights. The muffled distant whirr of his machine is the only noise in the room. Neville sits in the front row, forefingers pressed together and held up to his lips.

On the screen the images are jerky, in grainy black and white and with high contrast. Whitenesses play across the faces of the watchers. At the end of the film there is a black screen marked with scratches, flashes, possibly a number, odd squiggles that spark like neural connections, then a rectangle of brilliance. The projector whirr rises to a new tone, its empty spool revolving wildly.

Neville raises himself from his seat, crosses the starkly illuminated well of the theatre, and switches the lights back on. Then he faces the class. His voice echoes around it. 'There are obviously certain things you would wish to comment on,' he says.

He waits. No one interrupts him.

'About –' and he raises his hands, 'what? Objectivity? Structure, signs, meanings? But I want you to particularly think about the way in which the film is cut. The key word is *montage*. The film, remember, is by Kuleshov.'

One or two of the slower thinkers suddenly write down the name in their notebooks.

'Lev Kuleshov,' Neville says, 'wrote his first essays in film theory for a Moscow magazine. By the time he was twenty-one he had been given his own workshop in which he could demonstrate his theories. What you have just seen is a piece of film from those years. The face belongs to the actor Mozhukhin, later to appear in the French cinema under the name Mosjoukine. What has happened to that face; what range of expression does it have?'

Again, no one speaks; they all look as if they are not expected to.

'Griffith had shown how to assemble film dramatically. Now Kuleshov could show how, by juxtaposition, the meaning of pieces of film could be altered. You saw that just now. Imagine its impact in the early twenties. The actor's face is intercut with a plate of soup, and we see hunger, an attractive woman, and we see love, a dead body, and we see grief. But the face is the same. It doesn't alter at all.'

He looks round. 'It remains as it always was,' he says. 'Expressionless.'

A short while later Neville goes to his office and closes the door. On the desk top are two film magazines, a BFI dossier on David Cronenberg, and, under the anglepoise lamp, a telephone with a photograph of Marilyn Monroe stuck on its side. On the shelves are many books, carefully stacked, and several black and white blow-ups are fastened to the inside of the door. Posters for the Gance *Napoleon*, the Vigo *L'Atalante* and Oshima's *Ai No Corrida* are high on the walls. In one corner is an old publicity photograph of Gracie Fields.

Neville sits on a swivel chair of moulded plastic. He pushes it from side to side with his feet. He picks up the phone, puts it down, picks it up, dials.

During the conversation he asks, 'How much longer?' And then, 'Yes, of course I can.'

He stands up and goes over to the wallchart which records his comings and goings over the year. He has crossed and hatched and dotted and starred it with primary colours. He runs the end of his pen across it.

'Yes,' he says, 'I'd be able to make it.'

After a longer pause he adds, 'Well, I'd just have to make two journeys, that's all.'

He does not speak again for about a minute, then he says, 'Terry, I'm sorry; what else can I say?'

(2)

And now, the hospital.

The ward is late in opening. Neville sits and reads an Alain Resnais paperback until the nurse unfastens the doors and then he tags on to the end of the knot of visitors who walk down the central corridor. Groups peel away as they pass each ward. They carry bottles of Lucozade, bags of grapes, paperbacks.

Sylvia is in a private ward. The bed has retaining bars slotted into each side so that she appears to be resting in a metal cradle. Her nightdress is white. She seems lost in it. Most of the flesh has gone from her bones. She looks only just alive, a construction of tissues about to collapse and die. Even the bedclothes look heavy enough to crush her.

'My God,' Neville says.

Terry gets up and shakes his hand. 'Thanks for coming,' he says, 'I know it's a long way and you're a busy man. You needn't have waited outside. In cases like Sylvia's – well, they're a bit more understanding.'

Terry is Neville's brother. He has a thick but soft Lancashire accent. He is married to Sylvia.

'It's all right,' Neville says, sitting down.

Terry sits beside him. 'She's asleep, or unconscious, most of the time now. I can't tell which.'

He pauses, opens his hands, looks at his brother, then down at the floor. 'She's too young for this to happen to.'

But there is no youth about Sylvia. That too has gone. Instead she looks curiously ageless, as if the disease had driven out all her characteristics as it occupied her body. Only her red hair, which has been brushed, her perfume, which is strong, and the touch of lipstick, which is bright, tell of her age. And across the right eyebrow is a purplish-black bruise.

'She was pleased her hair grew back. You should have seen it a year or so ago. It's the treatment, you see, makes it fall out. She was proud of her hair.'

'Yes?'

'Right proud.'

'And the –'

'I know. She tried to get out of bed. They do that, you know. People who are dying. But she had no control, she just toppled on to the floor. That's why the sides were put on the bed. That bruise is nasty. They're a bit like wings, aren't they? The framework of aeroplane wings. Makes it look like a half-dismantled cage. Or a half-built one.'

'Yes.'

'There was no point in letting her harm herself.'

'Can't they find some other way?'

'Drugs, you mean? No. She's got enough pumped into her. This is the best way.'

'She must still want to get out.'

'It's impossible. I think she accepts it now.'

Even the nose has been pared down. Sylvia's nostrils are like a leper's. There are black patches under the eyes and her neck is as brittle as an unwrapped Pharaoh's.

'She wanted to go home, Nev. That's why she did it. She told me that. Up until a couple of days ago she still had moments when I could understand her. But you get confused over when things happened. You know what hospitals are like. You lose all track of time. Time is completely artificial in here.'

'Like film,' Neville says.

'What?'

Neville shakes his head. 'It doesn't matter.'

'She'll die here. It won't be long.'

'It must be an ordeal for you.'

'I can take it. You have to, don't you. I mean, you're my older brother, and you aren't even married, but you know what's going on. I can take it. But I can't understand it.'

Neville nods.

'I just sit here or beside a phone. It goes on for ever. You expect death all the time but I'll still be shocked by it when it comes.'

'Does she know?'

'She's not stupid, Nev.'

'I know.'

'You used to think she was slow. Didn't you?'

Neville said nothing.

'You used to think we were all slow. Not up to your standard, like.'

'For Christ's sake, Terry. That was a long time ago. I'd hardly grown up then.'

'I remember it, though. I'll never forget it. I know you're

clever and all that, and you're a couple of years older, but that never gave you the right to look down on people like you did.'

Neville starts to say something, gets out only the first syllable, and then says nothing.

'Sorry, Nev.'

'It's all right.'

'Shouldn't say such things.'

Neville puts the tip of his tongue between his teeth and holds it there for a few seconds.

'It doesn't matter anyway,' Terry says, 'stupid little things like that aren't important. Look at Sylv. Nothing much matters anymore to her. She's at the end, now. After her there's no one.'

'The end of the line?'

'No one to pass things on to. Her dad feels like that. Somehow it would lessen the blow if there was another generation. It's like us. We're the last of our line, as well. I don't suppose either of us would have children now. Wouldn't our Mam and Dad have loved that? There was a chance. Once. But she lost it.'

'Oh?'

'When you were in America. She lost it. Just one of those things.'

There is silence for a while between the brothers. Sylvia's breathing can be heard, thin, shallow, almost undetectable. It is the only sign that she is still alive. In all the time Neville has been in the ward she has not moved.

'What was it?'

'A boy. She didn't want anyone to say anything about it. Felt it was bad luck to talk about it. It was our secret, like. Ours.'

'Sure.'

'If only there could be something of her left,' Terry says, 'something I could get hold of, hold on to. Something more than old photographs.'

He is quiet for a while.

'Memories,' he says, 'that's all I have left. Everything else is being taken away.'

They look at Sylvia. Her eyeball trembles slightly beneath its lid. Her breathing is almost beyond hearing. The cold light coming in from the window makes everything seem pale, almost bleached.

(3)

Look, you can see that, high on the wall, just over the picture-rail, is a pair of horns, and beneath them a wooden plaque with the inscription *Royal And Ancient Order of Buffaloes*. Around the walls? A mirror with decayed silver backing; five photographs, framed in dark wood, showing rugby league teams, and two showing cricket teams; a silver trophy, slightly tarnished, in a glass case.

There are mahogany coat-racks just inside the door and the mourners shake and brush their hats, coats, scarves. Flakes of snow have fallen on the floor and are turning to water. Many of the men and women are rubbing their hands, blowing, stamping their feet. Some gather at the fire. It's a coal fire, lit half an hour ago, but it's warmth has not yet reached the far corners of the room. Someone picks a pine quarterlog from a scuttle and puts it on top of the coal. The wood catches fire quickly and begins to spark.

Several of the men say they'll have a short, just to warm them up; others have carried their pints upstairs from the bar.

On the long table in the centre of the room are rolls and sandwiches filled with tongue, cheese, egg, tinned salmon. There are sausage rolls, pork pies, bowls of pickled onions (brown ones, mind you), crisps. And fancy cakes with icing on the top that has been sprinkled with diced chocolate vermicelli, or had a cherry or a couple of Smarties stuck there. And a couple of tarts, one apple, one plum (tinned) with Carnation milk to pour all over them, and two big rich dark chocolate cakes oozing with cream. And hot tea poured out of giant pots by girls with bared forearms.

Terry has bought Neville a pint of bitter, which he sips.

'A bit delicate with that, Nev.'

'It's a long time since I've drunk it.'

'You used to be keen enough. People understand, don't worry.'

'I can hardly remember anyone. Who's that, over there – I know the face, don't I?'

'Used to live three doors down from us.' Terry stands close to his brother and whispers the identities of several of the mourners. Neville nods, keeping the glass up to his face. 'You really are forgetting us,' Terry says.

'I'd forgotten how everyone looks. As if you're all part of some natural process – families, jobs, living conditions, whatever. You belong to the same set. I feel –' He stops. 'Studied,' he says.

'Some of them think you've gone a bit strange. But don't you worry about it. They think that about everyone who moves out.'

Sylvia's father is a retired pitman with a shock of white hair. He looks as if he has bathed twice a day for the whole of his life. His cheeks are red and healthy.

He stands in front of Neville and looks him up and down.

Neville coughs.

'Neville, is it?'

'How are you coping?'

'Oh,' the old man says, 'I'm all right, lad. Many's the person who has a heavier cross to bear than me.'

'Tough times.'

'There've been none tougher.'

'Sorry.'

'Don't you worry yourself, lad. There's nowt anyone can do about it, anyway.'

'No.'

'Good beer, eh? Real stuff. They say London beer's as weak as water.'

'Really.'

'That's where you work, isn't it? London?'

'Well, just outside, actually.'

'I were down there once. When we had a good team, you understand. Things are different now.'

Neville nods.

'What do you do?' And the old man raises an empty glass to someone at the opposite side of the room, who nods. 'He'll get me one,' he says, 'don't you bother.'

'All right.'

The old man laughs. Terry, who has been talking to another mourner, turns back to them. 'I get hungry,' says the old man, 'it's terrible, I know. I couldn't eat owt before the service, but now that it's over I'm starving. I could eat a horse. Our Sylvia wouldn't have wanted me to starve meself. She liked life. She would want me to live as much as I could. Not shut meself away. Things like that can't be altered no matter how much we may want to. Those sausage rolls are nice. Do you think we're all here?'

Terry fingers a new black tie. 'Almost,' he says, 'there's another car to come and then we'll get started. Are you all right?'

The old man nods. 'You?'

Terry shrugs. 'Coping.'

'You're doing well, lad. Our Sylvia would be proud of you.'

Terry nods, puts his hands up to his eyes, then shudders and smiles back at him. 'Best see to that lot,' the old man says, indicating a group at the door, and Terry walks over to them. 'He's a good lad, your brother. Strong. You'll know that.'

'Yes,' Neville says.

'What was it he said you did? I tell you what, I could do with a cup of tea as well as this. That cemetery were really cold. Snowy sort of wind, as well.'

'I lecture in film.'

'You do what?'

Neville cleared his throat. 'I lecture in film. I do a course at a poly.' He pauses, then adds, 'It's a kind of university.'

'What do you have to do for that, then?'

'Well, students examine film culture. Analyse certain

works. Find out the grammar. It's a kind of higher criticism, really.'

'You mean like those reviews in the papers?'

'Well, it's a bit deeper. There's a thing called the Kuleshov effect, for instance. We have to try and find out how it works. It's a way of looking at how things are put together.'

'Our Sylvia used to love the pictures. Do you remember?'

'Yes.'

'Went all the time. I sometimes think she thought life should be like a film.'

Neville smiles. 'It's how a lot of us got interested.'

The old man shakes his head. 'Fancy that. Mind you, I couldn't be bothered with owt like that. Fancy me paying taxes just so as people like you can sit around talking about pictures. I don't know. Still, it's your job and you've done very well out of it, I hear. Maybe I've just got old, that's all.'

Neville says nothing.

'Pictures that we all used to go and see before they closed the picture houses down,' Sylvia's father says. 'It's a funny old world, that's for sure.'

Later, after he's had his tea, he will buttonhole Neville again. Neville will have his fingers, sticky with cream, fastened across a large wedge of chocolate cake he said he didn't really want to eat, but someone gave him anyway. As he raises it to his mouth the old man will say, 'Go on, Neville, you're pulling my leg. Talk about the pictures! What do you *really* do?'

(4)

And Sylvia?

As a child she sat transfixed in humming darkness among rising rows of spectators. Brilliance, blacknesses, colours swept across the screen and lit their faces like ghosts. Sylvia was open to it all – to those giant flawless faces with astonishing eyes; to those vistas of plain and mountain and desert, with tiny figures crawling across them; to hopeless battles where handsome men breathed their heroic last, and women luscious with romance yearned forever for them; to worlds where everything was possible, and most of all fate; to smoke, fire, ice, and waves crashing over rocks. Out under the red Exit sign, down the headlong stairs, through the burst-open double-doors and the night was thrilling, charged, mysterious, and as full of possibilities as a magician's cloak.

Life, home, the condition of growing up, all seemed tangential. The true substance, hidden but sensed, lay just out of reach. Head teeming with stories and stardom, Sylvia felt romance as the explorer, lost in blackness, hears through the cave wall the unstoppable force of the underground river.

And if she married, as she did, an old friend who was good and honest, but without ambition and with no desire to be *different* – why, the life of the imagination did not suffer. It thrived.

She was not neurotic, and neither was she inadequate in her dealings with the world. Not she. Sylvia was sane, practical, and adept. None could have faulted her. And even if her imagination did insulate her from disappointment, and at times despair, she could still face life, and death, with courage.

For in only one thing did she waver; her affair with Neville. If *affair* is the right word, for that applies not only the clandestine (and it was certainly that; Terry was never to know), but also mutual passion.

Sylvia had hung on to her fidelity with all the determination of tensed arms, gripping fists, closed eyes. All she needed was for someone to tell her that if she let go she would float. Neville whispered in her ear. She let go, and fell.

They were no longer the same. Neville had moved not only geographically but also intellectually and, she thought, morally. She found nothing in him to give her the adventure and excitement she had expected. This was not Romance, not even Life. She could forgive him for not understanding her sense of guilt and anguish. But she could not comprehend his lack of love.

Afterwards she wrote him long letters full of passionate

declarations. She had too much sense to send them, but too much imagination not to write them. They flared with emotion and imagery. She played the part of the forbidden lover, the beautiful loser. Page upon page came from her. How she wished they could melt together like clouds, burn as one like a red-hearted fire. How in death they should become not bodies but stars, points of brilliance in an inky-black heaven. She pretended that fate coursed through her.

Neville was in America when she lost the child. She asked Terry to say nothing. She knew that Neville, if he found out, would think it had been his.

It was, of course, Terry's. She knew that. And then came the disease.

It was possible to see all this as some terrible drama of retribution, of fate working itself out through betrayal, loss, death. She was proof of the coldness and violence of ancient justice. Artists were in tune with myth. They understood such things. It had been in all the films.

When she knew she was dying she put the letters on a coal fire, watched them curl, blacken, spout flames. It was enough that they had been written, and fitting that they should die with her. Nothing else was necessary.

For the last few weeks she was in a stupor of drugs and pain. She did not know that many, including Neville, came to see her for one last time. She knew very little. Just vague shapes that became more grey, less distinct; muffled and unaccountable noises that became less and less clear. The doctors declared an end at a certain time; they even wrote it on a form. For them the moment was distinct. But for Sylvia it was tentative and uncertain. Just a slowing down, a withdrawal, a fade. There were flashes, firings of nerves that became less and less frequent, a collapse to black, and then nothing – huge, profound, limitless, for ever.

(5)

A grey, formless void, without depth, from which undefined

shapes emerge. You cannot tell how, or why; and there is no sense of direction.

Some movement; perhaps a realignment of the frame.

Now the direction is down; in close-up they're grey, but further away the shapes are white, drifting, smaller. Snow. And beneath them, a perspective without colour, a preliminary design, a sketch. Like charcoal marks on paper which recede, maybe bend. But they're hills. Yes, slopes; the even, silent geometries of fields. You can see the hedgerows powdered with snow, the solid black squares of farm buildings with walls dusted white.

Lower, closer, and the farm passes beneath us, its roof sliding out of vision.

Look; you can see the town. Snow lies across the rooftops of the grey terraced houses, it carpets the slopes of the spoil heaps, obscures the marker lines on the football pitch and the car parks, it edges up road signs and bus shelters. You can see how it is carried down the streets and piles up against windows and doors, taking the colour from everything. It clings to the walls of the school, the supermarket; it covers cars, gardens. You can see it drifting everywhere.

And, if we lower further as we pass across the town, we can glide past the pithead. Its black silent headgear wheels, spokes and inner rims edged with snow, slide away to one side.

And now a screen of thorns with bare winter branches, and a few scattered trees, and a depression that forms into a small valley.

Snow gathers in the trees, covering rocks, reeds, the path. Move down the path, only at head height from the ground. A figure is walking towards us through the whiteness. It is dark-coated, almost a silhouette, its face and hair are blurs.

Close in now.

Neville walks towards us. His hair is wet with snow; it gathers on his coat. Closer still.

The face is expressionless.

Great blurs of snow fall between it and us. Sometimes the flakes land on him and he brushes them away from his face.

As tight as possible, on the eyes.

Neville's eyes are gigantic, clear, staring right at us. Blurs fall across them. One lands on an eyelash, the snowflake turns to water, trembles, rolls down and out of sight. The eye blinks, just once, then stares dead ahead.

PRACTICAL LIVING

I'M HALF-WAY through a residential course when the animal arrives; I'm at that curious midweek time when one feels tagged by procedure and nostalgic for home. Every evening, at half past six, I ring. This time Jean answers almost immediately. I press one finger against my earlobe and move as far as I can into the plastic bubble. 'Everything all right?' I ask.

'Yes, you?'

'It must be hard work. Are you tired?'

'A bit.' I can hear the kids shouting in the background, and Simon's voice becomes nearer and more excited.

'Hold on, Simon's got something to tell you.'

Almost before she has finished his breathless voice is saying, 'Dad we got something today.'

I know what it is before he tells me, and am angry that my reservations and warnings have gone unheeded. 'What's that, then?' I ask.

'It's a rabbit, a small white one with pink eyes. It's lovely. Uncle Joe came and we went down town and bought it. It's really nice, Dad, you'll like it.'

Joe again, I think. 'Oh good,' I say, without enthusiasm.

'We brought it home in Uncle's car, and we've got it some whatsitcalled . . .' I can hear Jean prompt him against one of Emma's monotonous chants. 'Sterilised sawdust,' Simon continues triumphantly, 'and it's been a bit frightened and shivery but it's settling in now.'

'Great,' I say, and when Jean is back on the line I say to her, 'I thought we agreed not to get one just yet.'

She laughs, making light of my displeasure. 'We weren't

going to, it just happened. You know what Joe's like. He got the hutch so he had to get them the rabbit to go with it. I was as surprised as you were.'

'Well,' I begin dubiously.

'It'll be all right. The kids are having a great time looking after it, they really are. Even little Emma's excited about the whole thing. And I'm sure Andrew will love it.'

Ah yes, I think, Andrew.

After I've used up my last ten pence I sit on the grassy bank by the ornamental lake and wonder about the rabbit. Ever since Joe turned up with the hutch in the back of his van I've waited for this to happen. I have tried to dampen enthusiasm by saying how awkward rabbits are, how they need constant feeding and cleaning even when it's pouring down, how they become a duty rather than a pleasure. Simon knew of my reluctance, but it did not deter them; he and Emma would speculate on an imaginary pet, imagining what colour it could be, what name they would give to it.

Some ducks waddle across the grass towards me, searching for food. They're sleek, fattish ducks who stand quacking a few inches from my feet. They, I decide, need no looking after. I can take pleasure in watching ducks.

I reach home after a long drive. Simon sees me first and runs down the drive, Emma following him. For a few moments I think that they are the only things I want in life. I can tell that they are both itching to take me to see the rabbit, but I first must embrace Jean. She tells me Simon fell at school today and grazed his knee, but that it's nothing to worry about; Emma is fine. 'And Andrew?' I ask.

'I saw him last night, after you rang. He's okay.'

Simon has rushed to the back garden to check on the hutch, and now he comes back. He is wearing a blue and white striped teeshirt and his fair curly hair looks as if all Jean's combings and brushings have had no effect. He's full of an infectious energy which Emma, too, is developing, although at the moment she looks merely impish. When people talk of our family's attractiveness they never mention Andrew.

'Dad, Dad, are you coming to see the rabbit?'

'In a minute, Simon.'

Emma pipes, in repetition. 'Dad, Dad, are you coming to see the rabbit?'

I have to say the same thing. 'In a minute, Emma.'

'We've been thinking of names all week,' Simon confesses.

'You know what they did?' Jean asks. 'They had me looking up a Thesaurus for words like *white* and *snow*.'

'We don't like Whitey, but we think Snowy's quite nice,' Simon says.

'And have you decided?'

'Not really. We don't know if it's a boy or a girl, you see. And we need a name that fits.'

I allow myself to be led to the hutch. Emma gives little dance steps of excitement and I feel mean because I cannot return their feelings. The hutch is against the back wall and faces down the lawn. Inside, the rabbit looks more or less as I expect it to look, small, white, indistinguishable from others. Simon opens the wire gate and reaches in before I can dissuade him. 'Come here, rabbit,' he says, and lifts it under its belly, bringing it towards him. The rabbit holds its legs stiffly and its tiny feet brush along the sawdust and dropping-covered floor. The ears are flattened back from the skull and its bulbous pink eyes stare unmovingly from their sockets. Simon holds it out to me. 'This is Dad, rabbit,' he says.

I stroke it because I know I'm expected to. The fur is surprisingly soft. In the sunlight it seems almost hurtfully white and its eyes full of mild blood. 'Daddy hold it,' Emma chants, and Simon hands it over. I am surprised at how light and soft the animal is. Uncertain and a little panicky when it leaves Simon's hands, it now accepts its position and lies, trembling quietly along my forearm, twitching its nose as I stroke the fur.

Jean has come out of the back door and is standing in the evening sun. 'You must look after it,' she tells the children, 'no silliness, now.' I lift one of the rabbit's ears and examine the tracery of veins within the coral-pink skin.

'We're feeding him and cleaning him every day,' Simon says, and I note the *him*.

'It looks as if it needs cleaning now,' I say.

'We swept it out this morning. Uncle Joe says it will take a few days to settle.'

'Oh yes?'

Simon nods sagely. Joe is uncompromisingly practical. He services my car, mends washing machines, does the odd bit of building work. He talks constantly of building his own house; when he tells me this he looks pityingly at me because I cannot do this sort of thing. I am sure that he blames me, and my faulty genetics, for Andrew.

'Does the rabbit make much of a mess?'

'Sometimes,' Simon replies, dubiously.

'I don't know anything about their diet.' And the other thing I'll have to find out is whether it is really male; I wonder if it's difficult to tell.

'Joe says to feed it carrot tops, things like that,' Jean says, 'and we have some grain from the pet shop. Simon thinks that Andrew will love him – don't you, Simon?'

Simon grins and takes the rabbit back from me, cradling it in his arms so that it will be safe. In his eyes I can see the careful solemnity he had when first we brought Emma home as a baby, a look that shows he has been admitted to the company of those who care for living things.

'Be careful,' I say, and he nods as if it was not necessary to caution him.

Although I have not wanted to look after a pet, I decide that I must do it as best I can. If I care for the rabbit then it will, I think, make it less likely that it will catch a disease or die or, by some remote chance, breed. The next day I go into town and buy a book on how to look after them. I read about general health, possible illnesses, and how to sex them. On the way back, following a chance remark about a cartoon that had been on television, Simon decides to call the rabbit Bugs. He does not now doubt that the rabbit is male.

Over the next few days we look after it dutifully. Before I go to work, and Simon goes to school, we open the hutch, sweep out the droppings, scatter fresh sawdust. We clean out its dishes and give it new greens, grain and fresh water. We keep an eye on the droppings to make sure they do not become too soft, which would mean that its diet was incorrectly balanced. I try to sex it by turning it upside-down and peering between its legs, but it wriggles and kicks and anyway the pink excrescence in the fur does not resemble either of the drawings in the book.

I discover that it does not get dirty, as I thought it would, but that it systematically licks itself clean, often with closed eyes. We also discover that Joe's advice about holding rabbits by the ears is wrong, and that one should only steady them, letting the weight rest on the hands or forearm.

I even begin to call it by name. I'll say, 'Hello, Bugs,' in the morning, as it presses against me, nose twitching because it knows it is food time. 'Time for bed, Bugs,' I say at night, closing the hutch. There's an old fireguard I put around the hutch to protect it from curious cats or dogs, and I raise this like a barrier each evening.

Over the next few days Bugs grows quickly. When we take him out of the hutch and place him on the lawn he seems happier, and nibbles at flowers and plants omnivorously. Every now and then he runs a short distance, starting and stopping abruptly as we hold ourselves in readiness in case he makes an attempt at escape from the garden. Also he makes leaps, or kicks, in the air, almost like an exaggerated nervous twitch, which makes us smile or giggle. When the time comes for him to go back in, Simon will say, 'Come on, Bugs,' and Bugs will settle down behind his wire mesh with no apparent complaint.

The only thing that bothers us is his ear; his right one. It has a tendency to droop or even flap down the side of his head, as if the tendons had softened into uselessness. Some days it's okay, on others it lies across his head as if it has no life. We try not to worry, call him Loppy-Lug as an alternative name, and tell ourselves that the nerveless ear is heredity's stamp on Bugs. Nevertheless, we're relieved when Joe examines him and pronounces him only mildly ill. 'It's a cold, that's all,' he says, 'he'll be all right in a few days.'

Afterwards, I get him on his own. 'You really think so?' I ask.

He shrugs. 'They're pretty susceptible to all kinds of things, that's the problem.'

'You don't think it'll die, Joe?'

He laughs. 'Not just yet,' he says.

And in a few days Bugs is indeed perkier, although the bad ear fails to match the balance and liveliness of the other.

Simon looks forward to showing Bugs to Andrew. He mentions it several times in the car as I drive to the home, and I try to discourage him. 'I don't think Andrew will be able to appreciate Bugs the way we do,' I say.

'Oh I don't know,' Jean replies, 'he'll be quite excited in his own way. I'm sure of it.'

Andrew is waiting for us, sitting in a chair with his good clothes on. Jean and Simon talk to him as if he is a baby being encouraged to speak. They tell him how they're glad to see him, how he's going to have a good time, how they have a surprise called Bugs waiting for him. Even Emma is picking up this habit, and constantly interrupts to try to tell Andrew things.

I struggle to lift Andrew into the car; he's a dead weight and is growing bigger. Jean sits beside him as I prop him up in the back seat. One of his hands moves erratically, describing broken arcs in the air; Jean holds the other. When I start the car he gives a mumbling, shapeless noise, which Jean says is one of pleasure.

On the return journey I watch them through the mirror. I can see Jean look at Andrew with the concern and love she will show during the whole weekend. Already I know that, on Monday, she will be distressed that we have to return him; she will say that when Emma and Simon grow up we should maybe have Andrew back. I won't say much, because she knows I think Andrew will be dead by then. In the mirror I can see the angle of his head alter, and his eyes move as if some bearing has become displaced within them. Already his face, handsome as a boy, is showing a numb bluntness. It is as if the alertness that character- ises his brother and sister is being made featureless by the pointless growth of his body.

At home we wheel him into the back garden, where he sits squinting in the sunlight. 'Would you like to meet Bugs, Andrew?' asks Simon. As if he has received an answer, he goes to the hutch and takes out the rabbit. 'Come on, Bugs, meet your brother,' he says, and gently places him on Andrew's lap. He does not let go, however, but holds the rabbit there. 'Do you like him?' he asks.

'Of course he does,' Jean says.

'He's lovely, isn't he?' Simon asks.

Andrew's hand rises, but slips back again, this time on top of the rabbit's white fur.

'You can tell he thinks he is,' Jean says, reaching across to stroke Andrew's hair along his forehead, 'don't you, darling?'

Over the next few days the family devotes itself to Andrew. We clean his teeth, brush his hair, cut his nails, take him to the lavatory. Jean prepares special food we can spoon into his mouth, the excess being carefully wiped from his chin. We select certain television programmes (cartoons, or those featuring wildlife) and place him in front of the set as if he appreciates them in the same way as Simon and Emma. Jean even reads him stories, tales of Jack who slew the giant and the squirrel who rode on a raft to the owl island. We take him into town, pushing him through the precinct and letting him watch the sunlight in the fountains. Jean buys him sweets and some new clothes; she decides that he can wait until his next visit before she need buy him new shoes – those he is growing out of are almost new, and will come in for Simon. On Sunday we take a picnic to a local wood and Andrew sits with us on the wooden seats while Simon and Emma try to dam the little stream with rocks and turf.

Each night we dress Andrew in his pyjamas and I carry

him upstairs. He's noticeably heavier and I find lifting him a lot more difficult than it was a year or so ago. We say goodnight but Jean always stops to tell him about whatever he has done that day, and will do the next day; before she kisses him and tiptoes out she makes sure there is a teddy bear on the pillow next to him. We leave a nightlight on in case he gets scared and becomes difficult to handle.

When it's time for him to go, I lift him into the car and say, 'Come on, sunshine; don't worry, you'll be back with us soon.' The drive back is always quiet, the air subdued by our separation. I cannot agree with Jean's contention that Andrew is sad. I can see no sign of emotion in him and tell myself that our affection for him makes no difference to him. Physically his body responds to warmth, comfort and cleanliness, that's all.

Within a few days Bugs's ear starts to give trouble again, and flops lifelessly down the side of his head. A sore appears on the end of his nose. Simon is worried but I tell him it's just a cold, although I can see him brood about Bugs's sudden lack of interest in the garden. Jean and I have a discussion about whether or not we should lace Bugs's food with a minimal amount of brandy; I'm not sure but Jean finally does this and Bugs, to our surprise, eats the food hungrily. Over the next few days we feed him on grain with a little whisky dashed over it, but cut down on the greens because his droppings are not as dry as they should be. Jean smiles and claims Bugs likes the new diet; Simon and Emma stick their fingers through the netting and comfort him as if he could understand what they were saying.

The treatment appears to do no harm; the sore above the nostrils scabs over, dries, and is gone within a few days. In its place there is a small blemish, a dampish depression as if the flesh will begin to scab again. He even regains interest in the garden.

Joe arrives one day and, before I can tell him not to ask, Simon wants to know his advice. We look into the hutch and Joe scrutinises the rabbit as if he were a vet. 'Yes,' he says, 'I see.' I wonder how much he really knows, and how much is mere bluff;

he has already been proved wrong, to my satisfaction, on how to lift rabbits. 'It's mild flu,' he says, then glances round the garden and pulls a tall weed from the edge of a flowerbed. 'This'll do him good,' he explains, folding the weed so that the sap runs down it then pushing it into the hutch. 'Milky-thistles,' Joe explains to Simon, 'rabbits love them.'

The next day the weather is bad, the continuation of an unseasonably wet and windy night. During the next few minutes when the rain appears to be easing Jean gets up from the breakfast table and goes to open the hutch. When she comes back I can tell that something is wrong. 'Bugs doesn't look too well at all,' she says.

'What's wrong?' Simon asks, getting up from his half-eaten toast. I reach out a hand to restrain him. Already I'm thinking what I shall have to do should the rabbit die.

'He's just lying in his hutch,' Jean says.

'He's not dead, is he?' Simon asks, turning white. Emma repeats the same question in a sing-song.

'No, no,' Jean says and, obviously wondering if she has been too emphatic, 'he just has bad diarrhoea, that's all.' The milky-thistle, I wonder.

'I'll go,' Simon says, and makes for his coat and boots.

'Sit down and finish your breakfast,' I say. 'I'll see to Bugs.'

Breakfast is unpleasant from then on. Jean is concerned, Simon worried, and Emma, perhaps sensing change, bangs her spoon and tries out several nonsense sentences. But I'm determined not to be rushed.

After breakfast I put on my old blue anorak with the loose zip, my boots, and go outside. The wind is cold and carries flurries of thin rain. Simon stands in the shelter of the back door, waiting for my report.

Bugs hasn't touched his food and is lying in an almost-sleeping position at the back of the hutch. His back legs are drawn up under him and his head is on his paws. His eyes look weary and are almost closed, and the troublesome ear lists helplessly across his head. At his rump and under his legs there is a nearly liquid mess of excrement, so much that it seems to be simply running out of him. I rake my fingernails across the wire but he does not respond. The rain suddenly gusts so heavily that I have to run to the back door.

'It doesn't look too good,' I say to Simon.

The morning is spent in a suspension of apprehension; I read the Sunday paper, Emma trips over my feet, we look at the puddles gathering in the road, and Simon goes up to his room to read. None of us really mentions Bugs, but on two occasions Jean goes out in the rain to check him and returns shaking her head. After lunch she goes out again to put some scraps in the dustbin and when she comes back I can tell that he's dead.

'Gone?' I ask, and she nods, plainly upset. It's strange how she has grown accustomed to the rabbit. I close the door on Simon and Emma, playing in the next room, and try to be brisk and efficient. 'Well,' I say, 'I'll have to bury him, I suppose.'

'In the garden?'

'I can only use that space between the lawn and the wall. Beside that plant, the one that grows a lot. If you go and visit your mother you can take the kids. I'll do it while you're out.'

'Do you want me to ring Joe?'

I shake my head. 'I'll do it.'

When we tell Simon his face sets for a few seconds then loosens in dismay. 'I'm sorry, Simon,' I say, 'there was nothing that could be done.'

'We'll get another one,' Jean says, trying to comfort him, and he nods. I can tell that, for him, no other animal will ever be quite the same.

A minute or so later he goes upstairs. We leave him undisturbed and prevent Emma from following him. For Emma this death is unique, and she repeats 'Bugs's dead, Bugs's dead' over and over again, her incantation testing the shape of this new event.

'How do you think Andrew will take it?' Jean asks.

I shrug. I don't think Andrew's grasp on memory, imagination or reality will be such that he will be able to even recall the rabbit. 'I don't know,' I say, evading the question.

'I hope he won't be too upset,' she says, as always thinking Andrew more capable than I believe him to be.

I'm glad that the rain has eased when I drive the family round to Jean's mother's on the other side of town. Simon is still assimilating his loss, but Emma is bouncy and aggressive. Jean has to act as peacemaker and judge. When they reach their grandmother's the children go running up the path. I arrange with Jean to pick them up later. 'Will you manage all right?' she asks.

'Doesn't bother me,' I say.

I drive back, then, with some trepidation, walk on to the back lawn. A fine drizzle is in the air and the side of the hutch is soaked. Inside, Bugs is lying on one side, his head thrown back, his legs extended. His pink eyes stare at nothing, and his hindquarters are stained a watery brown. I go for a spade and walk to the bottom of the garden.

The soil is sodden and difficult to lift, but I succeed in digging a deep narrow hole between the edge of the lawn and the small back wall. I load the dark earth on to a wide board left over from some wall panelling Joe did for us last year. In this way the soil can be tipped from it so that it will slide back into the hole. I congratulate myself for using this primitive but effective device.

After this comes the transfer of Bugs from his hutch to the bottom of the hole, which is deep enough to have touched stone. Handling the dead rabbit is something which fills me with apprehension and a little nausea, but I've worked out that I can maybe move him without actually touching him. This involves the use of Emma's beach things, a red plastic spade and a large yellow plastic bucket. I get them from the garage and crouch in front of the hutch. Then I open the door and wedge the bucket between the underside of the door and the ground so that Bugs will slide out over the edge and into the bucket. I grasp the spade and attempt to move him by placing the blade behind his shoulders and pulling him towards me. It's not very efficient mechanics but I'll not have to touch him; he'll fall headfirst into the bucket with his back legs sticking out of the top.

The blade's blunt edge pushes into the fur and, wanting it

over with quickly, I angle my wrist and pull Bugs towards me. I can tell by the force through the red plastic shaft that he's stiffened and his inch-long slide across the floor is heavy and awkward. I pull the blade away quickly, as if I have been given a shock, and drop it on to the grass. Bugs's body lies among the sawdust and food scraps, his eyes open, his legs out. His floppy ear has stiffened like a wing.

It is only now that I feel really sorry for him. He doesn't seem to have had much of a life, and what little there was has been defined for him by us. I can't treat him like this.

I go and get a fluorescent orange trolley that belongs to Emma's toy tractor. I wedge it against the door and gently get hold of the fur. Once the initial force has been applied he slides easily from the mouth of the hutch and into the trolley, slipping effortlessly into its hollow. I take the trolley to the bottom of the garden, holding it carefully as if I were cradling something of great value. 'Come on, sweetheart,' I say, and lower Bugs into his grave so that he doesn't have far to fall. The rain soaks my hands. Bugs, once tipped out of his trolley, looks suddenly white at the bottom of the hole.

Now I want the whole thing over with. I tug the board closer and my feet slip on the grass, scoring it with mud. I strain to lift the whole weight of the earth. The board bends, I think it's going to break, and then the dark earth landslides into the hole, burying the animal out of sight. I take the wet spade and lift the remainder of the earth on to the grave, then trample it flat with my boots. The rain becomes heavier, streaming out of the sky. I feel better than I have done for years.

TRYING TO GET TO YOU

AT FIRST I didn't recognise him. I had expected neither twin nor double, but this man did not appear to resemble his image at all. The hair was too soft, the nose too long, the frame too spare and the lips too thin. But of the five people who came into the room he was the only one who could possibly have played the dead singer. Apart from the girl, the others looked even more ordinary. The girl had her hair pushed back into a spiky orange comb; there were large metal rings dangling heavily from each ear, and a small tattoo had been printed on her neck, just under the angle of the jaw. She sat down in a chair while the others dragged their instrument cases into the room. Looking tired and heavy-eyed, she put a hold-all across her knees and leaned on it with her arms extended in a dancer's pose, both gawky and graceful.

I stepped forward to their leader. 'Jesse Aaron?' I asked.

He stuck out a hand. 'Mr Rivers?' I could feel the bones beneath the skin. 'It's an honour,' he continued, 'thanks for asking us.'

It's always difficult to judge height on stage, but I was surprised that he seemed so much smaller than when I had seen him six months ago. And yet he had convinced the audience within a few seconds.

'It's our pleasure, Jesse,' I said. I had wondered what to call him. Jesse Aaron had two first names but no surname; that was implied by the others, and hung invisible about him, a ghost always about to materialise, making itself manifest and real.

'The pleasure's mine.' The accent was a poor impersonator's Deep South, the kind of drawling mumble I had thought he would not wish to affect. 'Everything's fixed, uh?'

'Just as you specified.'

'The lights?'

'Just as you said. Do you want to check them?'

'What about the hoarding?' asked the girl. Her lips were partly open and I could see the sharp glint of metal fillings at the front of her mouth. Jesse looked puzzled, and glanced at me. 'You should have taken a look, like me,' she went on, 'there's a huge hoarding, must be twenty feet high, right over the stage.'

Jesse turned back to me. The other musicians stood around uncertainly, without starting to change or unpack. 'Is that right?'

'Look –'

'I don't want to be upstaged, Mr Rivers. Not even by him.'

'*Especially* not by him,' the girl said.

I sighed and pushed back my hair with my hand. My fingers touched the bald spot at my crown and I withdrew them sharply. 'Look,' I explained, 'we had it shipped in specially. It cost a lot of money. It took us years to find it, even; a lot of people thought it had been destroyed. And it took us an age to lash the thing up.'

'I want no distractions.'

I was thinking out my defence. 'Well, lesser performers might think it a distraction, that's true. Some impersonators –'

'He's not an impersonator,' the girl snapped.

'That's my point. Only impersonators could be scared of it and feel it dwarfed them. All of us here know you're not an impersonator. *Anyone* can do that.'

'I'm much better than that, am I?' he asked, aggressively, but I could tell he needed to be reassured.

'Of course,' I replied smoothly, as if there could be no doubt. One of the band members turned to a mirror and began to preen himself, but still there was no attempt to unpack.

'It's a tribute,' the girl said, 'a tribute to him.'

'Elvis just got there first, that's all,' Jesse said, sullenly.

'Sure.'

'I move in the same way, I phrase the same. A kind of accident, I suppose.'

'Or a gift,' the girl said.

'You never see impersonations done in front of originals, do you?' I asked. 'Tributes are *always* done in front of things like that. It gives them an extra edge, a further dimension.'

No one moved.

'Of course,' I said, 'we could have it moved. But that would take all evening, maybe more. And we couldn't mask it, if that's what you're thinking. They all know it's there.'

'Leave it, Jesse,' one of the guitarists said.

He stood silently, undecided. I noticed his jaw move as if he chewed gum, but I was sure there was nothing there.

'We could scratch the performance, if you want,' I said, 'but we couldn't pay you. You realise that.'

'This is blackmail,' the girl said, and turned to me. 'You're a real cunt, aren't you?'

'Look,' one of the others said, not taking his foot from the drum case he had it braced on, 'this guy could blacken our names on the circuit.'

'Would I do such a thing?' I asked, being careful not to look at the girl. She was the volatile part of this chemistry. 'Don't you think you should just go ahead and do it, Jesse? It'll be great. I know it.'

He hesitated for a moment, and then became suddenly decisive. He pointed at the girl. 'You, go with the man and make sure everything's okay. I don't want that thing to be fully lit.'

The girl stood up. I began to follow her out, but Jesse took me by the arm. 'You should have told me,' he said.

'I didn't think it would bother you.'

He appeared to consider this. 'It doesn't. But you should have told me. You weren't to know I would be so understanding about a thing like that.'

By the time I had caught up with the girl she was already at the head of the hall, gazing up at the hoarding. At this distance, the legs looked as broad as treetrunks. I stood to one side and looked at her, trying to be surreptitious, but she knew I was watching. I found her exciting, more so than I could rationally explain. Her figure was not particularly attractive – if anything, she was scrawny. Her hostility didn't arouse me either. But there was something about her that spoke directly to the senses, even though I wondered if she despised me so much she would want to lead me by a chain.

'What's that up there?' she asked. I looked blank, but she caught me with a harsh glance and I gave up trying to fool her.

'It's a screen. We show a lot of his films, you understand.'

'It's the kind that can be lowered, then. It would come down right in front of this. It would have to, otherwise you couldn't show anything.'

I nodded. 'You're right. And your friend Jesse Aaron would be on a thin strip of stage, not much broader than a shelf, and be plastered up against a white, highly reflective background that would give so much dazzle that no one would see him.'

The girl stuck her hands down the front of her jeans and hooked her thumbs over the waistband. She moved away from me, her heels clunking against the boards. She had a tired, pinched face, with poor skin and a darkness under the eyes as if she had not slept for nights. But the hair was alive, a bright, wiry orange that shone in the lights. The tattoo, though, looked dirty, the colour of decay.

Beyond the stage the convention droned, hummed, clattered. All the seating arrangers were busy in the hall. It was important to get the seating right; the hall floor was flat and the stage not high. In previous years I had received complaints from members unable to see. This year we had moved the sidestalls so that more seats could be fitted lengthways across the hall. What remained of the stalls had been stacked at the back of the room, but all the traders had taken away their wares – posters, videos, badges, books, memorabilia, records, photographs, teeshirts, plastic and plaster models.

'Okay, *Deke*,' the girl said, stressing my name unpleasantly, 'can we get the lights sorted out?'

For the next twenty minutes or so I worked with two volunteers to arrange the lights so that the hoarding would be bathed in a soft, muted glow while Jesse Aaron would stand in etched-sharp illumination. At the end of this time the girl insisted she should check the effect from the far end of the hall. 'You can see what you want from here,' I complained, tired.

'It's my job,' she retorted, and left me.

On the night before the convention opened I had walked back there myself. Along with several others I had assembled the hoarding like a gigantic simplified jigsaw, bolting its huge rectangular components together against a steel backing frame. We had all walked silently back from the picture to admire our handiwork. Presley scowled back at us, a two-dimensional colossus. Now, viewing it from beneath, I saw the figure as a pyramidal abstract, the legs surrealistically broad, the trunk narrowing to a comically small head.

Jesse Aaron's lights came on suddenly, catching me in an incandescent glare. I could sense the convention out beyond it, watching me. I felt weak, numbed by the heat and brilliance of the bulbs; I was unable to move, unable to see.

By the time the girl returned I had pulled myself together, and was exasperated and a little feverish. 'All right?' I asked sharply.

'It'll do.'

'It'll have to.'

The girl went away and came back with one of the guitarists and the drummer. They assembled the drumkit and checked the microphone leads. I went into the audience and talked with some old friends, apologised for the slight delay, and said the wait would be worth it.

When I went back to the dressing room it was full of a rich spicy smell. The other guitarist sat with the stub of a handrolled cigarette between his lips, a pair of tooled cowboy boots on the floor beside him. I felt a momentary panic in case we had a policeman in our audience.

Jesse Aaron was relaxed in a chair, a white cloth draped across his chest and around his chin. He looked like a man in a cowboy film who is about to be shaved. His eyes were closed and his feet were stuck up on a bench in front of him. The suede shoes were white, buckled, and unscuffed. The girl stood over him making up his face. Already the hair had been darkened and swept back; the eyebrows, too, were now almost black. She carefully applied lipstick to his mouth so that it began to look more sensual and full.

I stood uneasily beside them. The girl glanced up at me and then back down at her work. The face looked like a mask of Elvis, stylised and lifeless.

'Everything's ready when you are,' I said.

Jesse lifted one hand and let it fall, like the benediction of a weary pope.

'They're filling the seats now. We're a little late. But everyone is very excited.'

'If we hadn't had that hoarding to worry about we'd have been on time,' the girl said, 'we're professionals. All of us.'

Jesse said nothing. The rest of the band had dressed in shirts with embroidered pockets. The guitarists cradled their instruments touching the strings with an odd unfamiliarity, as if they were nervous of them.

'Almost ready,' the girl said. She made one or two final touches to her work, then drew the cloth from Jesse Aaron like a magician at the climax of a trick. Jesse got to his feet and looked at himself closely in the mirror. He was a caricature Presley, but he peered at himself as if he could see his dead twin. Then he shook himself loosely like an athlete before a race.

'You'll introduce me,' he asked, 'like we agreed?'

'The very words.'

'We're used to an audience that has been warmed, Mr Rivers.'

'Can't you hear what we've got on the speakers? Duane Eddy, Bill Black, the Ventures.'

'Yeah, yeah,' he said hurriedly, 'fine. Let's go.'

I went ahead of him and stepped up on stage. The records stopped and the audience, realising what was happening, began to whistle and applaud. The microphone stand was a slice of silver cut out of a pattern of gloom. Despite myself, I shaded my eyes against the light. I could see the convention ranged around the stage, the light catching their heads and the backs of their shoulders so that they looked like layers of moonlit waves, or a shallow rake on a cataract. 'Ladies and gentlemen,' I said, and my own voice came back at me, huge and strange, 'as you know, each year we like to present something a little special for everyone's enjoyment.' I cleared my throat and over the speakers it sounded like ripped cloth. 'We celebrate Elvis Aaron Presley, and because he was such a giant, so unique, we celebrate him in different ways.'

I could sense expectation building in front of me like a wave. All they expected were banalities. Only the banal was strong enough to hold the heat of their passion.

'What we have tonight is a celebration of Elvis, in action, on stage.' Applause began to break out, spasmodic and nervous, and I have to raise a hand to still it. 'When Elvis was born,' I went on, 'he had a twin brother who died.' I paused for a moment, then continued. 'The performer we bring you tonight has taken the name of that brother.' The darkness and glare were alive with tension. 'No one, *no one*, has more right to that name than this man. Ladies and gentlemen – *Jesse Aaron!*'

I flung out my arm, the audience roared, the lights were cut off, the safety lights swirled like distant fireflies; I made my unsteady, half-blind way from the stage. Someone coming on to it knocked into me as I left. Nothing happened, but still there was the roaring noise from the audience, with a few eerie screams being heard above it.

In the heated noisy dark I could see shapes move among the amplifiers on stage. There was a low whoosh over some mikes, and then the voice of Jesse Aaron rasped out the words that were like keys in the locked hearts of everyone out there. *Well since my baby left me*, he growled, *I found a new place to dwell*. The lights blazed up and the band were away, pulsing steadily, heavily. Jesse Aaron was among them, fixed like an enemy on wire, held by crossed searchlights. He was Presley from head to toe – black hair that fell thickly forward, a sneer, a red kerchief, ornately casual clothes, a guitar slung on his hip. It had all the drama of the expected. A moan of excitement and grief passed through the watchers. Someone began screaming, experimentally at first, then with increasing stridency and confidence. Anyone would have thought that Jesse Aaron was for real; we were all prepared to forget death. We reached out for him as people reach for a guide.

And he could do no wrong. He was raucous, tender, threatening, joyous. He swivelled, jack-knifed, struck postures like a stripper. He struck the guitar strings on downstrokes and pointed it at the audience like a gun. The crowd cried for more. He sang *Don't Be Cruel* and three women at the front raised their fists to their temples and trembled as if an electric charge passed through them. He sang *King Creole* and middle-aged rockers in drape jackets and crepe-soled shoes began to jive in the aisles with women in ponytails, stockings, and yards of petticoat. He half-crooned, half-recited *Love Me Tender* and many sat, as shocked as disaster victims, weeping softly. He took us through *Blue Moon of Kentucky, Hound Dog, In The Ghetto, American Trilogy*. He sang *Trying To Get To You, Trouble, Jailhouse Rock* until he was drenched with sweat and dark makeup smeared his cheeks like bruises. And he was gone before anyone realised it.

The audience clapped and screamed and shouted and stamped their feet, but he would not return for an encore. The house lights came up and they gradually began to quieten, falling silent one by one, all of them sweating, some ashamed, many happy. A few took several minutes to return to normal. A woman at the front, in high glitter boots and spangled cape, gave the last squeal of all and then looked round like a child astonished that everything about her had changed. Some were swearing, quietly but persistently and many wept openly. In their midst a young boy in the uniform of a GI stood with a puzzled look of anger.

Loss dragged at them like an undertow.

When I went back to the dressing room the band was slouched in exhausted postures. Jesse Aaron had a towel round his neck which was caked with makeup, and his hair stuck out from the side of his head in damp curls. The girl passed him tissues which he was using to swab his neck and face. The others sat with open cans of beer in their hands. The girl was taking off Jesse's shoes.

'The money, then,' Jesse said, tired.

'I'll make out a cheque.'

'Cheque?' The girl was stripping off his socks. As she did, her hand supported his leg.

'Every payment has to go through procedure. I couldn't pay you in cash. Sorry.'

He shook his head wearily, accepting the arrangement. 'See that the man gives you the right amount, will you?' he said to the girl.

She stood up and suddenly, without warning, he put out his hand and covered her crotch with it, his fingers pointing downward. She knocked it away. 'It'll wait,' she said.

Jesse Aaron smiled. No one else took any notice. 'You'll do anything for old Jesse, won't you girl?' he asked, his grin broadening, as she followed me out.

I felt a weak, feverish tremor pass through me. It seemed I was close to the real world of fame; a heady, physical world where outside morality did not fit and the body was pushed to the brink of disaster. Elvis, too, had been pushed to that point, then beyond.

She followed me to the little room I had as an office and sat in a chair, her legs slightly parted, while I unlocked the desk and wrote out a cheque. Our treasurer had already countersigned it. I almost made a mistake on my own name.

All the time I was aware of how close she was; how, under the clothes, her body was spare but effective. A comment from me, a question, an observation could propel me into that alien world. I held out the cheque, just short of her reach, and my mouth dried as I tried to think of something to say.

She reached out and took it from me, studying it carefully before folding it.

I cleared my throat. 'It went well,' I said lamely.

She made no effort to move. 'It usually does.'

'I think everyone was pleased.'

'Yes.'

She looked round the room, taking in all the para-phernalia of convention administration I had stacked and pinned on shelves and walls.

'He's too good for the likes of this,' she said.

I wasn't quite sure who she meant. 'Jesse, you mean?' I waited to see if she disagreed, then continued. 'He's got the most appreciative audience it would be possible to have.' I was used to defending the convention among outsiders; a comment like this, from what should have been a sympathetic quarter, was unexpected.

'It's a pantomime audience cheering its hero, that's all.'

'No.'

'Eternal adolescents, nostalgia junkies – you know I'm right.' She leaned forward. Her eyes shone with a kind of illness. 'Admit it; that's your secret fear.'

'We're like any other group that supports its cause. We're bigger and better organised, that's all. You wouldn't accuse people who liked jazz, or old films –'

'Look around. Everywhere there are pictures of him. Hillbilly farmboy, GI, gone-to-fat superstar; he's on walls, badges, screens. What you see are symptoms of a disease.'

I laughed uneasily, uncertain as to what she would do next.

'He didn't start off like this, you know.'

I nodded.

'He left himself behind somewhere.'

'He changed, you mean.'

'*Was* changed. We put Jesse Aaron together, he and I. We studied everything – postures, mannerisms, phrasing. Jesse Aaron was assembled from all those parts.' She paused, and her tongue protruded a little from the metallic teeth. 'Talent can't get through anymore. Because all you want is Elvis, or Marley, or Lennon, or Morrison, or Joplin. You don't want invention. You want a mechanical contrivance. Like Jesse Aaron.'

'You should be pleased. You must make a good living out of it.'

She nodded. 'We do. That's the tragedy. We've sold out for a second-rate parody. We call it *being realistic*. You're the same, Deke. You make believe you could have been like Elvis if only you'd had the breaks.'

'You're wrong.'

'You're all like that. Me as well. We all pretend we could have been the perfect sister, buddy, lover.'

'And twin.'

She paused, then added, 'We all think we could have saved him.'

We sat quietly for a while. I could hear one of his records drifting from the convention.

'You can't escape him either,' I said.

She did not reply, but I saw a small muscle twitch in her neck.

I went on. 'You've tried to break free as well, but you can't. You *are* like everyone else.'

She looked at me and her face was tensed, as if she controlled herself only with difficulty. Impetuously, I got down on my knees in front of her.

She took my head between her hands and gazed into my face, searching for something hidden. I felt my breathing become lighter and faster as I waited for recognition.

The girl pressed my head harder; I could feel the bones against my skull. She put her fingers to my eyes and pulled the skin so they widened. Then she moved the fingers to my mouth and eased it apart, pushing the lips and peering at them. Finally she lifted the hair above my ears and over my forehead.

Then the tension slackened, and she took her hands away. Slowly she shook her head. 'It's no good,' she said, 'you're nothing like him.'

She stood up and walked out of the room. I did not even see her go, although I heard the door clash shut; I was hanging my head.

Several minutes had passed by the time I got back on my feet. Elvis looked blankly at me from a calendar on the wall. Already the girl would be with the rest of Jesse Aaron's group as they loaded their instruments into the back of their van. They were already being borne away into the past.

I walked back into the hall, combing back my hair so that my bald spot was disguised. Records from thirty years ago blasted through the thickening air. Orange and blue and silver lights whirled and spun across the throng, and everything hummed and shook with excitement, memories, worship. The convention was as heady and as dangerous as a drug. Suddenly the lights went out but for a strobe. In flickering pitch and magnesium white it snapshotted men, women, children in caped jumpsuits, high-collared denim, cowboy shirts, glittery lamé jackets.

I watched for a while. Before long the dance would end and they would all settle down to watch the late-night film on the lowered screen. I went into the room where Jesse Aaron and the band had changed. Crumpled tissues and buckled cans littered the floor and the air smelled sour. I stood among them, not moving.

When I got back to the hall the film had begun. It was *Loving You*. Elvis rode into town on a jeep; he was dressed in working denim, and seemed bruised by his own sexuality. I found a seat and watched. Soon the country band's woman manager would sign him up, a poor orphan boy, to sing with them.

And soon, too, he would drive her to the deserted graveyard at night and ask her to direct the car lights onto the tombstones. There, chiselled on one, would be the name he had taken – you will see it plainly in the beams. On the giant screen Elvis will say how he ran away from the orphanage and took the name of this man here. He looks truculent, beautiful. 'This here is where the real Deke Rivers is buried,' he'll say.

And I'll sit there in the gloom, my lips moving in time to the soundtrack, and remember when I first saw this. For it was then that my spirit took a blow which crippled it for ever, and from which I would never wish to recover.

BLUE

'WE'RE CERTAIN it must be his,' she had said.

The day was hot. I could see the excavator from a mile away as it crouched on the flatland like a giant locust of yellow metal. We drove at an angle to it along a road as flat and exposed as a causeway until Nick swung the Land Rover off the road and headed towards the dig. Picks and spades clashed and shuddered in the back while Sally bounced on the seat beside me. Used to this kind of ride, she kept her balance better than I could. I thought I was going to crack my head on metal or glass.

At the excavation we stopped and clambered out. The air was monstrous with heat. The ground smelled of salt and thick, clogging mud, and all the vegetation was low and fibrous. It felt as if the sea could reclaim it at any time.

The team stopped work and stood awkwardly round the site like men discovered at a crime. Nick introduced me quickly and without formality, but none of them came forward to shake my hand.

'This is it,' he said simply.

It was strange to stand beside the opened patch of ground. The excavator shovel had scored it and clawed up long strips which lay, broken and dumped, next to our feet. Beneath the thick dark upper layer were patches where the soil was stained a vivid and surreal RAF blue. I felt heady. The blue was the colour of Asian gods.

'It's here all right,' Nick said. 'No doubt about it.'

I hadn't met him before. Sally had talked about him and, like a jealous father, I had sought from her aspects of him that I could criticise. Now he appeared to be more of an organiser than I had suspected ('a daydreamer' I'd scoffed, when I'd heard about his plans, but this was a considerable operation). He had a beard and tinted glasses and a forage cap. He wore jeans and turned-down Wellington boots that were caked with mud. Sally had told me he had a genuine flying-jacket which he wore at university, and a genuine RAF tunic he kept locked in a cupboard.

I sensed he knew I was unconvinced and resentful. Sally would have told him, anyway. That was why he was pleasant to me, and that was why he had already implied that he would consider any objection I would care to make. Yet it was clear that, in the end, he would let none of his decisions be swayed by me. Just as he would go his own way with my daughter, so, even if I objected, he would continue and finish the dig.

My father was down there.

Nick went to talk to the operator and the excavator restarted, digging its metal teeth into the wide shallow hole and gouging another solid layer of earth away with a long scraping scoop. The noise of the engine exploded away on all sides. Two of the team swept the earth with metal-detectors. The sun was so hot I could feel the blood move in my temples.

'We calculated all this,' Nick said. 'There was an eyewitness. You didn't know that, did you?'

I shook my head.

'He was miles away but on a good sightline. He just thought someone else would be doing something about it. We got hold of him almost by chance. A few days with the detectors did the rest.'

'Wasn't it reported?'

'You know how things go in a war. And by the time people got round to looking for it – well, it had buried itself. These days they'd be on it like vultures. Souvenir-hunters strip crashed aircraft within a couple of hours now. Even on mountains. And there's no doubt that it's down here. We've followed the scatter pattern very closely. A complete dis-integration would have been different.'

Sally came over to stand beside me. Her shirt was sticking to her; one of the team kept looking across at her but glancing down when he saw me watching him. It was natural enough, but I still had a complex reaction to such everyday glances; it was compounded of jealousy, protection, puritanism and a sense of being set free. On her relationship with Nick my feelings were even more contradictory.

'There's a kind of standard pattern to the way they crash,' she said. 'Nick's quite an expert.'

'So I hear,' I said drily.

'We found the impact zone a few feet back,' Nick said. 'The Spitfire would have hit here –' he pointed behind the excavator – 'and ploughed deep into the ground just here.' He indicated the excavator claw as it scraped and peeled the earth. 'We don't think it can have broken up all that much. There's a layer of harder subsoil over there. See the slight change in vegetation? That's a line of harder, denser soil. Well, rock deposition mostly, although covered with softer sedimentation now, of course. That probably brought it up short, concertina'd it.'

A metal-detector whined and from the dig one of the team picked a featureless twist of metal the size of his hand. He brushed the damp soil from it. 'Could be anything,' he said.

'The way I see it,' Nick continued, assisting his explanation with hand movements, 'he must have come back over the sea, at as low an altitude as he could maintain. We know the rest of the squadron went into a dogfight and that he was with them, but what happened after is anyone's guess. Officially, as you know, he just went missing. So he would come back in, probably low on fuel and losing it, maybe hit and wounded, maybe even being pursued – although we don't think so, for he was never claimed. He could even have been dead at the controls. He came in –' Nick's head sheared through the air – 'and hit.' He smashed one hand into the other.

I nodded. He pointed to some earth that was slipping over the edge of the grab. It clung together unnaturally. It was not the same consistency as the rest of the soil and did not take the sunlight as it should. 'Engine oil?' Sally asked.

Nick nodded. 'We're just above the point of rest. The

main body of the plane will have been gradually sinking. After all this time it could be a good way down.'

Enthusiasm took him and he held my sleeve as if wishing to convert me. 'Just picture it,' he said, and I knew he would be able to hold an audience just by the urgency in his voice, 'the Spitfire coming low and fast out of the sea, with the sun as high and as hot as it is today. Maybe the plane would be trailing smoke, maybe even it would be on fire, the pilot willing himself home and yet unable to make it –'

He broke off as if he had suddenly realised who he was talking about. 'Sorry,' he said, and I wondered if he was speaking to Sally rather than me.

'It's all right,' she laughed, 'even Dad didn't know him.'

'He may have baled out,' Nick said to me.

'And drowned at sea?' I asked. I was shocked at how bitter I sounded.

He shrugged.

'Or he may still be down there,' I said.

'I can't think about that,' Sally said quietly. Another piece of metal came up and she bent to examine it. 'What is it?' she asked.

Nick began to scrape the caked earth off with the side of one hand. 'It *looks* like a wing spar,' he said. 'Let's see . . .'

I looked out across the immense flatness to the distant sea. A pair of oystercatchers called in the distance. I couldn't help reflecting that this man who had gained control of my daughter was now, in a way both mercenary and perverse, gaining control of my father as well.

All that long afternoon they worked. I believe they expected me also to lend a hand, but nothing would have induced me to join the dig. I sat at a distance from it, both fascinated and repelled, sometimes tugging at the coarse tubular grass. It smelled of rankness, as if its existence was indifferent to any subtle ecology.

The sun declined across the land, swivelling the excavator shadow, but the humidity and the heat remained high. Twice I saw thunderclouds begin to form, and once I thought I saw distant lightning flash broadly and thinly across the horizon, but no noise came after it. On the next occasion we all heard a distant grumbling echo, like thunder, and raised our heads to an unexpected and temporary cool breeze. But the clouds broke apart under their own pressure and dispersed, and the heat continued to oppress us. Apart from a thermos of coffee they did not break from work but continued to dig methodically towards the plane. I'd placed a tube of grass between my teeth and it had tasted bitter, so I was pleased with the coffee even though it reminded me how hungry I was.

Every now and then a fragment of metal was unearthed – a piece of the fuselage, a strip of rotted aluminium, fragments of alloy that made the detectors whine and yelp. Even Sally took her turn at the excavator controls. Nick shouted up at her. She handled them with a confidence and skill that surprised me. I wouldn't have been anything like as good at them.

Hunger and the heat made me feel lightheaded. They must have felt worse. Nick was reluctant to give up for the night, but the light was draining out of the sky and that was obviously what he had to do. The trench was wide and several feet deep. The soil at its bottom had been stained blue with the rotted aluminium.

'One last scoop,' he said. They made it and unearthed the tip of the tailplane. It protruded from the soil at the bottom of the trench. I felt weak, loose-bowelled, slightly drunk.

The old inn (it called itself an hotel) faced the open landscape. It would be hard to live there in winter. Even in summer the building seemed dangerously exposed, the highest point for miles, its chimneys the first to be struck by lightning or bowled over by wind. Nick used it as a base. Approaching from a distance I imagined it deserted, but its remoteness and relative antiquity drew customers from miles away who raced to and from it at full throttle along straight flat roads. We sat in the bar with basket meals and beer. I was crammed between Nick and Sally in an unconscious parody of the position of guest of honour.

I didn't join in the conversation much. The others, made slightly drunk by the day, had lively but not very coherent discussions about aircraft 'recovered' (their word), about search techniques and disintegration patterns, bomb-detectors and metal-detectors, Mason's classification of locatable wrecks. Someone reminded Nick that he had promised to shave off his beard if this one was found, and everyone laughed when he tried to back out of his promise.

It was all a long way from my war. Mine was an abstract war. It could never be found among documents and memories and pieces of wreckage; it was located in the imagination. I thought of it in terms of grand abstractions and eternal principles – glory, heroism, triumph, grief, belief.

I was born after he vanished. All I knew of him were my mother's photographs and memories. His image stood in a frame on the sideboard. It was a studio portrait, with the photographer's name an extravagant flourish across a lower corner. My father is seen in head-and-torso shot, wearing his cap and tunic. The focus is soft, almost too soft. And, as was common at the time, in water-colour, handpainted and unreal. I remember that, not realising how it had been painted, I thought his skin incredibly soft and uniform, like that of a doll. His eyes are of porcelain blue, the blue of distant calm skies, their centres circular as targets. His uniform of RAF blue is pressed and exact, the golden wings as romantic as buccaneers' gold.

He had taken off one day and never been seen again. According to the books he was Missing Presumed Dead. The way my mother talked about it his disappearance had been mysterious, destined, even heavenly.

Later in the pub the talk turned to the lives everyone had mapped out after university. I sat still and said even less.

Nick took me round to the back of the inn across the dark courtyard. He unlocked the door to the old stables and it creaked sharply, as if rust would snap the hinge. 'You've got to keep it under lock and key,' he said, 'it's amazing what people will steal.'

There was no light in the stables. He directed a torch around the flaking white walls and on to a floor of uneven stone. Bits of my father's aircraft lay scattered across it with identifying tags wired round them as if on corpses' toes. When Nick moved the torch the shadows leaned expressionistically.

'You see how much we've got up already,' Nick said. I nodded. His face, lit from below, was washed with melo-dramatic highlight and shadow, like a fortuneteller's over a crystal ball.

'Don't think they're just being dragged out of the earth,' he said, 'no, we're doing a very professional job. I could show you a chart with all the positions noted. By the time we're finished it will be possible to draw an exact representation of this plane's breakup and scatter pattern. We plan to put it on a computer in three-dimensional graphics. It could be a great help.'

'To who?'

'Other diggers. Crash investigators. Farmers.'

I picked up a piece of metal and looked at the tag. The code it carried was meaningless to me. 'What would the other customers in the pub think of this?' I asked, testing the metal's balance and weight.

He shrugged. Under the beam the spars and fragments appeared to shift. 'Pieces of militaria for some. Scrap metal for others.'

'You see it archaeologically.'

'That's right.'

'Or maybe more like a grave-robber.'

'You shouldn't try and put me down so much. I can understand your feelings.'

'Really?' I asked.

'I see it all practically,' he said. 'Not romantically.'

I put the metal down.

'You think it's your past?' he asked. 'Your personal untouchable sacred past?'

'If it is I can't recognise it. It's too . . . substantial. Too tangible. I can't tell you what any of those pieces are or what they have to do with the workings of an aeroplane or what they had to do with my father's death.'

'I can name every one,' he said softly. 'Would you like me to prove it?'

'You needn't try to make me feel guilty,' I said. 'I don't feel I should know.'

He had already drawn from me more than I ever thought I would give. I was reluctant to confess that, although my rationalism told me otherwise, my imagination had never quite grasped the fact of the aeroplane coming *down*. Nick was right. In my mind my father had disappeared into the blue, melted into cloud. I had fed on all those postwar films in which handsome young airmen vanish into the skies. If he had ever come to earth then a shower of rain seemed more fitting than these poor beaten pieces of metal.

'I'm sorry,' Nick said, 'I should have realised you would take this hard.'

'I'm not taking it hard. I'm being very objective and reasoned and understanding about the whole thing.'

'Yes,' he said, 'sure.'

Back in the bar I felt compelled to talk. The long day had loosened my tongue. And I refused to let Nick buy me a basket meal just because he bought all the others; I would pay for my own. 'Take your chance now,' he said. 'I'll be a different person when the beard goes.' Perhaps I also believed the extraordinariness of the day had touched me with fluency. I sought out Sally like a man driven to confession. She sat there and listened while I talked about the war, about the courage of fighter pilots and the odds against them. I must have used all the old phrases. To me they were apt, exact and alive; to her they may have rung as hollow as lies.

'But you never knew him,' she said.

'Of course not,' I said, 'that's not the point.'

'Perhaps that's exactly the point.'

'I know enough about him. About his background. Where he was born, how he grew up, the university he went to.'

'You don't know what he was like as a person. He may have been someone you simply couldn't get on with.'

'He was only a young man.'

'He was about Nick's age.'

I sat and looked at my drink, aware as I did so that this

too was a formulated reaction, a cliché that she would interpret. Despite their apparent concern for me, I was little to them. An irrelevance. A hollow man, his skull stuffed with dated ideas, unfashionable morals. I was a jackal returning to a stripped and empty carcass.

'Why do you think I'm here?' I asked.

'That's easy. Because I told Nick that you just had to be here. You're part of the chain of events. And of the ritual.'

'I'm here because of a sense of duty,' I said. 'And you?'

'Because of Nick. And because he's infected me with his passion for old engines, deserted crash sites, all the paraphernalia of these . . . celebrations.'

'Don't you feel anything personal? Some link with that man down there?'

'*If* he's down there. We still don't know. No, I don't feel anything much for him. I feel more for you. I keep thinking of you as a character in some second-hand, careworn myth. I know who you are, Dad. I made the discovery years ago. You never had that advantage.'

She took a drink, and smiled quietly.

'Think about it,' she said, 'it's in all the best myths.'

'Whose idea was this?' I asked. I could hear my voice develop a sudden rasp.

'I told Nick a long time ago. He's been working on it since then. All the time coming closer and closer.'

'When you first told him, were you lovers?'

'No. It's what threw us together.'

I went to bed and couldn't sleep. The room was narrow and hot, and it didn't cool when I opened the window. For a while I watched the sky, waiting for a storm, but it had receded further. I could even see stars. You could navigate by the sky on a night like this. Far away towards the horizon the lights of an aeroplane passed in geometrical leisurely silence.

I sat on the bed and drew myself up like an unborn child but with my wrists on my forehead. I thought about him. About his photograph and about the heap of formless jetsam in the stable. At the edge of speculation I believed he would be here somewhere, sitting in the corner of the room with that exact blue uniform and filmstar skin.

Of course there could be nothing there. It was just another of my outmoded fantasies, my own hackneyed way of trying to cope.

I may have slept then. Certainly I conjured images as contradictory as a dream. I am reaching out, one hand splayed, through fire that crumbles like soil to the touch. I am reaching down into water or air to find nothing, to touch the rounded smooth skull of an ancient burial. The cockpit is empty, the pilot dispersed, dissolved, beyond touch or thought. We tumble his bones into a black plastic bag to await the coroner. As it lies beside an open grave a wind will fill it like a black sail.

An hour or so after going to bed I heard noises from the next room. It was Nick's room and I knew the sounds were of he and Sally making love. I pressed myself to the wall like a climber on a sheer face. I could feel their rhythm passing through it, vibrating steadily in a heavy, laboured pulse. While they coupled one of them would be braced, anchored against it. I imagined the force of their lovemaking absorbing itself into the fabric of the building, echoing down the walls and, fainter and fainter, vanishing into the earth.

I could hear their sighs clearly. They were light and high. I tried to imagine them together, but I had not seen her naked since she was a child and her body was as big a mystery to me as my own mother's. I stood splayed against the wall feeling my face become motionless, bloodless.

The climax, when it came, was low, almost unheard.

I sat back down on the bed. I had known they were lovers, had reminded myself constantly of that fact. But hearing it gave me a sharp and unhealable wound. It cut me with an edge of loss and passed time.

And there was also release.

When I heard her open the door I stepped out into the corridor. It was dark, secret. Her face was a pale smudge in the half-light, unformed. I took her arm. It was warm and flushed with blood. Her eyes were wide, both apprehensive and challenging.

I realised that she had wanted me to hear.

The landscape looks different at night. The horizon is closer, as if the earth is tilted around us and we are driving to the centre of a broad, vast, shallow bowl.

Sally drives the Land Rover quickly but efficiently. Picks and spades rattle in the back.

When we get to the site there is a cool, easy breeze blowing from the sea. The excavator stands beside the opened earth. Its colour has been bleached by the night and it looks less bulky. Deathly.

I look up. There are still a few stars.

We reverse the Land Rover until it stands beside the hole and then rotate the swivel light on its roof so that the beam is directed down into the disturbed earth. The plane's tail protrudes like a shark's fin. We start the excavator and Sally takes out great slices, wedges, slabs of earth from above the fuselage as I shout guidance.

Soon it is obvious that only spadework is left so we get down into the wound and start digging.

We work in a rhythm, clearing the soil away from the main body of the plane and piling it to one side. Sometimes the earth makes a dark sucking noise as the spade blades slice it, but it stays compressed in thick cakes like peat. And it always falls heavily.

The earth slips and makes soft, unreal noises under boot soles.

We come across bits of metal and softer, flexible material that could be anything. Decayed rubber, padding, clothing. We throw it to one side. We lob, hurl, cast aside the finds.

We wreck Nick's system as surely as the plane itself has been wrecked. I don't care if it's beyond recovery. I don't care that the scatter pattern will never be plotted, the computer chart never be made.

After only a few inches we smell the cold. It catches in the back of the throat like the cold of an opened grave. There are unrecognisable smells released from the earth – sharp, like cut metal, and rank, like lifted flagstones.

The lights throw mountains and gullies on the bottom of the dig. Some are ridged with blue almost as if a painter has walked the scar. At times we push our spades into smooth wells of blackness, as black as carbon, as pitch, not knowing what we are cutting into. The ground sighs. The ground is broken by us and reformed.

We bend and heave and sweat and wheeze. The spades strike, glance, scrape on metal. The tailplane juts up like a marker, a monolith. A blade.

Just before the dawn I see a figure walking towards us. It does not deviate from its path but walks straight towards us across the flat land. I can watch it coming at us in the thin but strengthening light. From its build, from its walk I can tell that it is a man. As he comes closer I can see that it is a man in an RAF flying tunic. Closer still and I can see his skin, given an unreal uniformity by the light, his face, which is cleanshaven and young, his eyes, which are wide and direct. He stands at the edge of the dig, without speaking, looking down, not entering. He is like a man outside a magician's circle.

The dawn comes up without drama across the distant unseen sea.

I turn away and push my spade into the blue.

MY LIFE AS AN ARTIST

LAST NIGHT she saw the dead child again. Cord still round its neck, it rose through her dreams and floated in mid-air above the bed, its tiny hands open as if to grasp her, its eyes accusatory in their glassiness.

I woke to her sobbing beside me. This visitation, which has occurred since the boy died, neither slackens nor becomes less immediate and painful. Every few weeks she sees it, and when she does it brings a fearful clarity and despair to our lives.

I do not like to think of how long we have been together, for it reminds me of how little I have achieved. It was many years ago that I first told her of my ambitions, mentioning names she claims she cannot now remember – the Armory Show, *tachisme*, the New York School. Our talk then was of success, of voyages, of fame. We were confined, restricted, but on the edge of greatness. I would take menial jobs, I said, and work at night or before dawn, but already I have supervised and maintained and policed this building for longer than I care to remember. The child, if he had lived, would have been a student by now.

She crouched on top of the bedclothes, her back bent so her forehead almost touched the sheets. From her throat came noises like an animal trying to vomit. I struggled up, weary, shaken awake by the force of her terror. Years ago I had tried to comfort her and been partially accepted. Now the thing has become almost stylised, an aggravation, a chore. I struggled out of bed. I had to go over the top of the bedclothes because they had been tucked in too tightly at the side; my pyjamas, which are too loose-waisted, slipped down my haunches and I had to grasp them beneath my belly to prevent them from slipping further.

'It's all right, it's all right,' I said mechanically, 'it's only the same old nightmare.'

She rolled to one side and craned her head to glare at me. Her eyes swam with tears and her face looked like tallow. 'It's not a nightmare,' she said between gasps, huge hungry gasps that sucked in insufficient air, 'it was him, as plain as day.'

I went to the kitchen. The linoleum was cold on the soles of my feet. These days, I always have a kettle full of water standing by, and a cup with a teabag and a spoonful of sugar in it. Much time is saved this way. I merely have to boil the water and add milk from the carton in the fridge.

When I returned, moving a little unsteadily so that the cup clicked in the saucer's recess, she was sitting up in bed with her head in her hands. Every few seconds her shoulders and arms gave a convulsive shudder, and sniffing noises came from her nose. 'Tea,' I said brusquely, placing it in her hand.

I got back into bed after loosening the bedclothes at the side. I could hear her drink, and feel her tremble, but I did not touch her. Soon I got further into the bed and looked the other way.

'It isn't a nightmare,' she said.

'When are you going to turn the light out? I need my sleep.'

'He's real. Why can't you see him?'

I said nothing.

'He's never going to let me rest,' she said after a while. 'Ever since it happened, he's never let me rest. Just when I think he's gone, he comes back to me. He's haunting me; he won't let me go. Why can't you see him?'

'Because he doesn't exist. Because you dream him, that's why.'

'Sometimes he's just there, hovering. It's as if he wants to hold on to me, as if I can stop him from dying just by reaching out and holding him to me. At other times it seems as if he wants to say something; his little mouth opens but no sound comes out. I can see tiny bubbles of spit at the corners of his lips. And all the time he has the cord wrapped as tight as a noose round his neck, poor thing.'

'What's it attached to?'

'What?'

'What's it attached to? The cord, I mean.'

She was silent for a few seconds. 'I don't know. It just sort of . . . disappears. Fades out.'

'Like the Indian rope trick, you mean.'

A few more seconds silence, then she said, 'You bastard. You heartless bastard. You're making fun of me.'

I did not move. 'No I'm not. I was making a comparison, that's all. Can't I do that? Won't you allow me to get things clear anymore?'

'You never did care for him, did you? He was just a *thing* to you, a kind of collection of muscles and flesh that you thought you didn't have much to do with at all, even though you'd fathered him. But he was our child, our *boy*. I'd carried him for nine months, felt him grow, felt him –' She stopped, made a choking noise, then continued. 'Felt him kick, up until those last few days. We had his cot, his clothes, we even had his name. He was a person to me. Even though he never really lived, he was a person.'

'He never had a chance to be a person. He had no personality, did he? There was nothing to distinguish him from any other male baby, was there? They all look more or less the same, anyway.'

'You say that because you don't want anything to do with him. But we could have saved him. It's true. If we'd done the right things he'd be with us now, strong and good-looking and giving us a purpose, a point.'

I threw aside the covers and got out of bed again, still clutching at my pyjamas. 'Christ, this was years ago. Why do you still want to torture yourself, and me as well? Nothing could have prevented it.'

'That's the difference between you and me. You run away from the truth. I have to face it.'

I shook my head and went to the kitchen. I poured myself a drink of milk.

If I had been a true artist, I thought, I would have

encapsulated that little scene in a few rapid charcoal sketches. My fingers would have darted, swooped, fluttered across the paper; the charcoal would scrape lightly, as dry as the sound of grasshoppers. There, on the page, would have been my wife, hunched forward on the bed, her vertebrae so clear on her back that they could have been numbered; here would be me, standing with weary features under the kitchen light. Perhaps, if I had had the nerve, the child would be there too, like a kind of anatomical drawing of the foetus in the womb, but with its eyes open, its hands stretched out, although, it seemed, no placenta at the end of its noose.

This morning she was still edgy, troubled; I could not resist making a comment about how tired I was, but she did not respond.

'I'm going to do some work today,' I said after a while.

'Work?' She was unsure what I meant.

'Yes,' I said, with heavy exaggeration, '*work*. Sketches, I think.'

'You haven't time for that. There are other things that need to be done first.'

'They can wait.'

'No they can't. You could lose your job if you don't sharpen up. I'm serious. People are talking. They expect things done.'

'Who? Who've you been talking to?'

'There are the side stairs, for instance. Everyone mentions them. They're filthy.'

'I didn't design these flats, you know. It's not my fault these animals can get in and sniff their glue and shit on the steps.'

'It's still your job to maintain things. No one else will do it; they know you're paid for it. Drawing doesn't pay anything. Nothing at all.'

'You're a Philistine, you. Always have been. You've never believed in me, have you?'

'What have you sold? Go on, in – what – twenty years, what have you sold? All those drawings, all that oil paint you had to buy, all those sheets of expensive paper for your watercolours – how much money have you made from it?'

'That's not the point, is it? Van Gogh sold nothing, and neither did Gauguin. They gave them away, just about.'

'You're not them. And all you do is spend your time doodling.'

'They're plans, ideas, theories.'

'They're things like interlocked hooks repeated over and over the page, like grappling irons stuck together, or fish-hooks, or bent propellers.'

I stood up, knocking over the stool I had sat on. I knew it would fall, and knocked it so that it would make the most noise. I saw her flinch and her eyelids close for a fraction of a second.

'Jackson Pollock's wife didn't say that to him, I'll bet. Or Mark Rothko's when he did big canvases of maroon on crimson.'

'I've never heard of them. And they sound terrible as well. Are they dead? People will buy anything, they really will.'

'Yes, they're dead. Like Duchamp and Braque and all the other people who were really, *really* important. Perhaps I'll be dead as well before I'm recognised.'

'Come off it; come *off* it. That's really wishful thinking, isn't it? There's no point in consoling yourself like that. People won't think, when you're dead, that they overlooked a genius. I know *I* won't.'

'Despair. We kill ourselves out of despair.'

'Who's *we*? Caretakers? Maintenance men? Grow up, you can't ever be an artist. When you think about it, that's obvious, isn't it? Go on, you can confess it to me.'

I shook my head.

She leaned forward, her voice soft but taunting. 'I'll not tell anyone. Promise.'

Again, I shook my head.

'Come on, love; we have to live with each other. Let's be honest, okay? Neither of us are going to do anything special. We're going to end our lives as ordinarily and as quietly as we lived them, slipping away in some hospital ward somewhere surrounded by other old people. There won't even be a son or daughter to see us go.'

'I don't want to end like that,' I said bitterly.

She reached out and put her arms round me. 'We have to. We're the kind of people who have no choice. Neither of us are special.'

She was holding me to her now; I wanted to break away, but could not. Despite all the years, all the arguments, I still found her a comfort, although I constantly denied it. '*I'm* special,' I said, in a last fluttering of protest.

She held my head to her bosom. I could hear her heart beat, and remembered how, once, I had been given an instrument to hold to her skin so that I could hear through it the heartbeat of my unborn son.

My refuge lies deep in the building, a secret place to which only I am allowed the key. I can, if I wish, have it blaze with light, or I can sit in the darkness with only the boiler's mouth showing its blue and yellow flame. I can think about my life, or my work, or I can sit and do nothing but lean against the pipes, feeling the throb of the pumps like the heartbeat of a massive giant. The people who live here think they know the building, but they don't. They know their own rooms, the main entrance, the stairwells. Only I know its lungs, heart, nerves. None of them has seen the cable, thick as a constrictor, that feeds them power, or touched the range of master fuses fixed to the brickwork like a black lattice of cells, or stood on the giant pipe that carries away the waste. And none of them has ever seen my work, or even suspects is existence.

I have it filed in the crates that once held spares for the plumbing. Often I imagine that, when I am dead, the refuge will be searched and my hoard discovered. Gradually, like delicate objects being removed from a dig, my sketches, acrylics, water-colours, oils will be carried out into the full light of the outside world. There they will astonish and delight a public who had never thought me capable of such grace, such finesse, such beauty.

Once or twice, carried away by this vision, I have toyed with bringing forward its realisation. I have climbed on the stepladder so that my head is just below the pipe that crosses the room just under the ceiling. I have had a length of electric cable stretched round my hand, but have never had the courage to even loop it over the pipe, let alone make a noose from it. I get down from the ladder with my legs trembling, and fold the cable, fasten it, and put it away.

Afterwards I sit in the dark, listen to the roar of the furnace, the click of the thermostats, the distant humming of the pipes. I like to think I am not in my refuge at all, but in the engine room of some great vessel that sails through unknown seas, carrying me ever nearer my destination.

I like to believe I'm actually going somewhere.

GUIDO'S CASTLE

As SOON as he arrived, Richard phoned from the airport. 'Hire a car,' Guido advised in his heavily accented English, 'you understand that I cannot leave her.'

When Richard drove off, the sun had risen across the hotels, the petrol stations, the hoardings. In front of a roadside factory an electronic display flicked up an extra red degree. It was going to be sultry; the pilot had warned them.

On the flight Richard had sat with the new paperback of *From The Watchtower* in front of him, but had found himself several pages into it without being able to remember what he had read. All that he had were vague impressions from his first and only reading, more than twenty years ago, and from the critical pieces published recently. After a while he just looked at the cover and, on the back, the photograph of his mother as a younger woman. Beneath the photograph were selections from reviews, all recent ones. Richard recalled the narrative as glacial and obscure, the tone as annoyingly haughty. Now his mother was praised as an articulate and uncompromising stylist, a writer's writer. He had hoped that the passenger beside him would ask about the book. He would have talked about his mother, but not mentioned Guido. Instead, she was only interested in whatever was coming through her earphones.

The book was in his case as he drove, firstly through the straggle of buildings that had grown up round the airport, then through the countryside. A strange sense of finality had begun to inhabit him. He was aware that he was about to witness the natural end to a life, and everything around seemed a counterpoint to this – the red-tiled houses with their shutters pinned

back, the occasional restaurant with striped awnings and its
outside table deserted at this time of day, the fields of maize and
the tiny vineyards, a patch of sluggish water beside the road with
birds darting among tall motionless reeds. At first it appeared,
too, that the day would continue fair, but as he neared the villa a
thick layer of cloud, its grey edge sharply defined, moved across
the sky like the closing of a gigantic shutter that stretched from
horizon to horizon. Before long rain began to fall, streaking the
dusty wind-screen and pattering inside the car so that he had to
wind up the window. Even enclosed, Richard could smell the
heaviness that the rain released – a mixture of silt, manure, grain,
flowers.

From now on he had to drive carefully, with the wipers
at full speed, and his concentration was such that he could not
look beyond the villa to see how the new building was
progressing. He was, in fact, slightly relieved to have arrived
without coming across a flooded road or skidding on its slippery
surface.

Guido was waiting for him. As soon as he saw the car he
came lumbering out into the rain, looking as if his wits were as
slow as his deliberate and heavy movements. He was wearing an
old suit, the one he had married in. Small enough then, it scarcely
fitted him now, and was fastened across the chest by only one
button. Beneath it he wore a collarless shirt, like that of a peasant,
which was open at the neck. His black shoes were splashed with
something the colour of flour which Richard guessed to be
cement. Guido's face, heavy enough at the best of times, seemed
to have lost some of its muscularity, and the flesh sagged under
his eyes and jaw.

Richard wound down the window. The rain increased,
and several drops caught him in the face and made him blink.
They had no effect on Guido, who stooped towards the car with
drops of water running from his bald scalp and dripping rapidly
from the end of his nose. 'She is still here,' he said, and extended
his hand.

Richard shook it perfunctorily; his hand always felt so
delicate inside Guido's. All around was the noise of rain striking

gravel, tile, foliage, and there was a muddy smell in the air, as if from an overflowing ditch. Dozens of bright-shelled snails had come out into the downpour and were crawling across the grass at the front of the villa. 'How long?' Richard asked.

'Now that you are here, I think it will not be long.'

'Today? You're certain?'

'My own mother died like this. I know.'

Guido reached for his bag but Richard took it inside himself. He had expected the villa to be in a state of disorder, with dust across the shelves, unwashed dishes in the sink, perhaps an invalid's dirty linen stuffed into a corner somewhere. Instead everything was tidy and in its place. After a few moments, though, Richard found the scrupulousness artificial, as if the rooms were exhibits in a museum.

Guido came with a towel and lifted it to Richard's face, but Richard took it from him and dried himself. As he handed it back he noticed that there were still drops scattered across Guido's coarse skin. He accepted the towel like a servant. 'She is in our room,' he said quietly.

On one side of the door were her bookshelves; on the other, the photographs that she had framed and hung on the wall. About a dozen in number, they were mainly of friends she had made when she had lived in London, and then Venice. One was missing. Lucinda had been known for her high critical standards as well as her novels, and had been unsparing on those she felt were doing slack work, even if they were her friends. After she married Guido one, in particular, had taken his revenge. In his latest collection of stories he had portrayed her as a blue-stockinged spinster, too aware of literary theory to be any good at life, enchanted by an obtuse and barbaric Sicilian peasant. Richard had sent her a copy, although he had not wanted to; he was afraid that she would find out from elsewhere. She had acknowledged it without comment, and the subject was never mentioned again. By accident or design, however, the author's photograph had vanished from the wall. And, to Richard's perpetual annoyance, there was only one of himself, and one of his late father, but there were two of Guido.

Lucinda was in the bedroom. A folding bed was packed into one corner, which Richard guessed Guido must now use. The blinds were half-closed, and the room smelled of antiseptic and, beneath that, a thinly fetid odour. Lucinda did not move as he walked in. She was lying on one side, with her grey hair carefully combed back and fastened with an elastic band at the nape of the neck. He had expected her to look mortally ill, but he was shocked at how senseless she appeared. Her mouth was partly open and the breath rattled in her throat like that of someone unable to spit. Her eyes were open, but stared straight at the wall; the one next to the pillow was heavily bloodshot and wept a little. Her hands stuck out from the side of the bed and made continuous picking motions, as if she was trying to unravel an invisible object right in front of her. When Richard tentatively touched them they grabbed his own hands ferociously and would not let him go. All the time the blank, senseless expression did not change.

Guido brought a chair and eased it behind Richard so that he could sit down. He was speaking in a low, comforting Italian, saying that Richard was here, that he had flown all the way from London just to see her.

Richard, uncertain as to what he should do, looked up at Guido, who raised a finger to his lips as if he anticipated a question which should not be asked. Richard swallowed, and said, 'Hello, mother.' He was self-conscious; if his mother had been able to respond he would, perhaps, have felt differently. As it was, he did not know how to act.

Guido began to move about the room. He rearranged the flowers and the get-well cards from those people still in contact with Lucinda. On the bedside table was a photograph of their wedding. In it, Lucinda hung on to Guido's arm whilst looking at him with evident affection and love. He stared at the camera as if intimidated, by jowls emphasised by the angular light, his best suit looking cheap beside Lucinda's expensive dress. Beside the photograph were what looked to Richard like small pieces of medical equipment – an empty phial, some packets of disposable rubber gloves, the top of a syringe, a heap of what could be wadding or swabs, a feeding cup like those given to babies. 'Should I leave you with her for a few minutes?' Guido asked.

Richard, apprehensive, shook his head.

Guido came over, stood behind him, then bent to whisper in his ear. Richard could feel the warmth of his breath on the side of his face. 'Be careful,' he whispered, 'remember that the sense of hearing is the last to go.' Then he moved to the opposite side of the bed and pulled up a stool. He looked far too big for it.

'I've brought you a new edition of *From The Watchtower*,' Richard said at last, 'it comes out next month, remember? There's talk of a profile on the BBC, and a couple of the heavy Sundays are going to do a write-up, I think. I've said I'll phone them when I get back. I'll tell them you'll be better in a while.''

Richard could sense Guido looking directly at him, but he dared not return the look. He thought, now, of the original article that had sparked a revival of interest in his mother's work. It all seemed a matter of chance, luck. From being ignored she was on the brink of becoming fashionable again. But what would he say when he was asked why, at the apparent height of her powers, she had stopped writing? Dare he say that she had found happiness with an Italian bricklayer ten years her junior, who had never read a book, let alone heard of her? He could not imagine how he would deal with such questions. In interview, Guido would come across as strong if simple, honest if unimaginative, straightforward if naive. Richard, on the other hand, felt that he himself might appear evasive, over-rational, mistrustful; that each of his replies might hint at hidden depths. He could come across as the jealous, embittered son, unable to understand his mother or her work.

'You would like the design,' he went on, 'it looks good.' He wondered about putting the book in her hands, but thought that her restless movements might tear it to shreds. '*The Cartographers* comes out in about six months.' He tried to ease away his hand, but she would not let go.

Richard cleared his throat. 'The first big review of the American edition of *Following The River* has just arrived,' he continued. 'I remember there were some fairly hostile comments on the first edition. Times have changed. This new man says that your prose is clear and lucid, and not cerebral at all. He sees you as part of the English Romantic tradition. I guess he's thinking of your themes – loss, separation, love. Outposts.' He did not repeat the comparison that had been made with Pound's *Cathay*.

Richard tried to think of other things to say. He felt foolish and embarrassed with Guido sitting there, but knew that, had he not been at the other side of the bed, he might not have had the strength to say anything at all. For he thought it not unlikely that his mother would hear nothing but a dull, incomprehensible murmur, indistinguishable from the sound of rain.

'It's pouring down,' he said. 'Can you hear it? It's very heavy.' And he thought of the rain sluicing down the drainage channels into the streams; he thought of the river turning brown with mud and bearing branches of trees, clumps of grass, the bodies of dead animals out towards the lagoon.

'There could be lightning,' Guido said, 'but it will be silent, I think, and pass away over the open sea.'

There was a long pause. Richard flexed his fingers, but still Lucinda clung to him. Guido did not move.

'You're still building that thing out at the back?' Richard asked, not wanting to lapse into total silence.

'Yes,' Guido replied.

'She used to call it your castle. When she phoned. *Guido's at work on his castle*, she would say.'

'She defended it. The authorities said it had to be dismantled.'

Richard nodded. Guido had been lucky to have Lucinda; she had been his champion, no matter what. Without her, his ludicrous building would have been piles of bricks by now. Secretly, Richard thought that, when the villa eventually came to him, he would have Guido's monstrosity demolished with the quickest possible speed. 'It isn't finished yet?' he asked, remembering the cement on Guido's shoes. He hoped that it was; the smaller the building, the easier it would be to deal with when the time came.

'I have the edge to do. I do not know the English word.'

'Battlements? Castellations?' Richard could not keep the dry sarcasm from his voice.

Guido nodded. 'It is the right height now. I had a little work on it this morning, just before you came. Lucinda was asleep.'

'Do they still say it is unsafe?'

'They have given up chasing us, I think. Anyone can see that it is not unsafe. I was a bricklayer; I build strong, sturdy things that will last for years. Your mother told me about the Watts towers in America. No one would pull those down now. They could not.'

When Lucinda had told Richard that Guido had begun 'a little something' at the back of the villa, he had thought it would be some kind of decorative work – a fountain, or an ornamental wall, something to prove that he, too, had ideas about structure, function, design. But, as her health declined over these last few years, the building had become massive. Gradually it had taken the shape of a turret, square in cross-section like a classical campanile, with enough space inside to live like a lighthouse-keeper if ever he decided to put in floors. Richard had last seen it earlier in the year; from a position further along the road, it appeared to be growing to dwarf the villa. Closer to, one could see scaffolding round the rim and a rough but efficient pulley system rigged to its side. Guido's ambition seemed to be to build his castle as high as possible. He had even dug around the foundations to strengthen them further.

'We must move her now, Richard.'

'Move her?'

'She must be turned so that she faces the other way. The doctor has told me I must do it. Will you help?'

Richard hesitated, then shook his head. 'You do it; you're used to it. Can you get my hand free?'

Guido came round and gently released Richard's hand. Once this was done Lucinda's fingers made odd, fluttering motions, as if they sought to mimic the unravelling that had so occupied them only a short while before. Guido began to speak in Italian again, in a gentle, almost lullaby voice that was full of endearments. Then he lifted the sheet. Richard flinched. His mother's nightdress had ridden up to her hips, revealing limbs that were the colour of putty and seemed to have lost all resilience in the skin. A plastic tube snaked from her groin and led to a stoppered bag at hip level.

Guido picked her up, cradling her so that she looked frail and breakable in his arms, and put her down on her other side. From her mouth came a noise like a broken snort. Then he rearranged the nightdress, lifted her head a little while he plumped the pillows, and put back the sheets, folding them with a careful precision.

'A little drink,' he said, and raised her head again, this time to drip liquid into her mouth from the baby cup. Lucinda did not respond at all. Her bloodshot eye, now uppermost, stared dead ahead. Guido lowered her and wiped her mouth with a towel. 'It was fate, Richard,' he said suddenly, 'her work was destined to become famous.'

It was chance, Richard thought; chance, and ambition. Someone had wanted to promote an obscure and out-of-fashion writer and, in so doing, establish himself. Lucinda had been lucky that her books had been there at the right time.

'She should have carried on writing,' he said, 'she shouldn't have stopped.'

Guido was taking a length of black elasticated material from a drawer. 'She told me she did not want to say anything else. She wanted to keep silent.'

'Things could have been different without you, Guido.'

Guido smiled, seeming not to take this as a challenge. 'It is pointless to think about what might have been. We must think only of the present, and the future we are building with it.' He passed the band around Lucinda's arm and tightened it. 'Do you wish to see this?' he asked.

Richard looked dumbly at him.

'She takes a little by mouth, in the drink you have just seen me give her. But now I must also inject her. The doctor said this could be arranged, but I said I would do it.'

Richard shook his head but watched, repelled and

fascinated, as Guido filled the hypodermic. The amount seemed terribly large, unnecessarily so.

His face must have registered shock, for Guido turned to him and, in a voice that was almost fatherly, said, 'Please remember what I have said.'

Richard got to his feet and walked out of the room. He felt shivery and a little faint, for he was scared but also excited. He knew that he would not have the courage to do what Guido was doing. Outside the rear window, which was patterned with droplets, he could see the pale bulk of Guido's castle rising from a spray of rainwater.

After a minute or so Guido came back through. He had a swab of linen-like material in one hand and was wiping the other with it. 'She is comfortable now,' he said.

'You gave her all of that?'

'It has been agreed. Everyone understands.'

Richard's voice was high with excitement. 'That much morphine? You're killing her, Guido.'

Guido lifted his hands, then shook his head, as if the accusation made no sense. 'It is the only help she can be given. I have seen her suffer stroke after stroke, each one crippling her more severely. It was like watching a building at night, with someone going from room to room, switching off the lights. She has been dying slowly, and in much pain. Do not accuse me when I have to help her.'

Richard looked back at the castle. Against this landscape, its pallor had an unsettlingly surreal quality. 'Officially, then, she'll die of something else.'

Guido put a weighty hand on his shoulder. It felt intrusive but reliable. 'She is drowning. Her lungs are filling so she cannot breathe. The morphine is a kindness.'

Richard edged away so that the hand fell from him. 'That's how you know it will be today.'

'I waited until you came. To let things go further would be cruel.'

Richard walked to the back door and opened it. The rain had lessened, and he could see that around the turret there was a heap of bricks, a cement-mixer, a mound of sand, a tarpaulin covering what looked like bags. A thin waterpipe of green plastic, attached to a tap on the outer wall of the villa, lay coiled along the ground. 'God knows how this will affect the value of the property,' he said.

'You and I will be her executors. You know that?'

'Yes. And I know that this place is yours until you die, and most of her money is yours as well. Until you spend it.'

'I need no money, Richard. Enough for my food. And this is almost complete. You need have no worries.'

'You must have exhausted yourself working on this. All those bricks to haul to the top, all that cement to mix.'

'I hired friends to help me. They were good workers, but very cheap. Lucinda approved.'

'Guido, tell me – why did you build it? I thought at first you were trying to make a point, possibly trying to join some kind of exclusive brotherhood, but now I don't think that is the reason. I can't see the point of it all. In all probability the castle is doomed. Lucinda won't be able to protect you now.'

'You must help me, Richard. It is important.' Guido shuffled his feet and looked down. 'I have read all of her work,' he said.

'I don't believe you.'

'Oh, I did not undertstand it – not in the way that you would understand it. But I read it all, and I read all the articles that you sent. She did not care anymore; she said she wanted to be forgotten. She had nothing much to say when her books began to be published again, just as she had nothing to say when that man tried to make fools of us both in his short story. I made her take his photograph from the wall. I would not have our honour insulted, not even by his image.'

'I didn't realise. No one ever said.'

'Why should either of us have said? For Lucinda, the past was no longer of importance. And you and I could not have talked about her books. I have nothing to say about them. You would be too clever for me. You would have read one again, on the plane.'

As Guido spoke the rain cleared, quite suddenly. It seemed as if the rear edge of the cloud had slid from the sky above the villa and was now racing away towards the sea. Richard looked up to see trails of white cloud, like streamers, spread across a blue sky. The sun came out, and almost immediately the ground began to steam.

'I'll make sure that her gravestone mentions that she was a writer, Guido. I'll even make sure that it mentions you.'

'Gravestone?'

Richard turned to him, puzzled. 'Of course. She comes from a small village, originally. There's a space ready for her.'

'She did not mention that. Sell it, Richard, or keep it for yourself. Lucinda was precise about what should be done with her. She wants her ashes scattered in the lagoon.'

Richard had crossed it many times. It was a thin lake of weed, of silt, of sewage, criss-crossed by ferries and speedboats, ringed by eel traps. Often there were carpets of greasy foam slicked across its surface, and always there was the rank, muddy smell of decomposition. For years now it had been said that the lagoon was dying.

'We must hire a boat,' Guido continued, 'and not let anyone know what is happening. A few flowers, thrown into the water afterwards, will be enough.'

Richard shook his head. 'She never wanted that.'

'You can see it in the will. There can be no doubt.'

Quite suddenly Richard felt cheated and angry. 'Did you influence her as much as that, Guido? She always wanted to come back home, and yet now she wants to be scattered in the lagoon? What did you tell her, that she would form part of some process, turn into a cloud, eventually come down as rain? This is all your doing, Guido. She could have had money, fame, perhaps even greatness if she'd carried on writing. Instead she wastes her last years with you. Instead of spending time with like-minded people, she spends it with a bricklayer. She ruined herself – no, *you* ruined her.'

Guido, to Richard's surprise, nodded. 'Often, Richard, this is what I think myself.' And, with a half-smile and an apologetic shuffle, he moved away and walked back into Lucinda's room.

Richard, still angry, and still wishing he had been even more accusatory, walked outside into the sun. He could smell water vapour; all around him steam rose from pools of rainwater. He pulled at the tarpaulin, which showered him with droplets, and discovered that there were several bags of cement underneath, resting on a wooden pallet. The sand was drenched, but warm to the touch. And he could not resist bending to straighten out the loop in the plastic pipe,

The turret had been built with an arched space in its flank to which no door had yet been fixed. Richard stood with his hands on the support pillars, then went inside.

The turret was open to the sky, with a shaft of sunlight reaching part-way down its upper levels. A sturdy metal ladder was fixed to the wall, and several ropes hung from the upper rim. The floor was littered with broken brick, scaffolding wood, metal clips, torn bags; everything had been dampened so that there was a fusty smell of decaying paper, damp sawdust, wet mortar.

Richard did not plan to climb. He disliked ladders, and was aware that this would make him a laborious and ungainly climber. Then he thought of Guido, ascending quickly and gracefully despite his bulk, and put his hands, then one foot, on the metal rungs. He steadied himself for a few moments, then began to climb. At each step he told himself he could stop, and go back. Several times he did stop, imagining that the ladder was pulling away from the brickwork, but then he persuaded himself that he was safe, and could take a few more steps. Because he had read that one should never look down he kept his eyes fixed on the rungs and wall just in front of his face. He was surprised when he reached the top.

The summit of the turret was a grid of metal clamps and rods, with cement-edged planks placed across them. Richard almost bumped his head on the lowest one, then found that he could flatten his body against the ladder and edge between it and the plank. Suddenly, in front of him, there was a thin ridge of parapet and then, dizzyingly, a huge expanse of sky. Richard eased his body upwards a little further. Most of the sky was now blue, but towards the lagoon the raincloud had a dark, bruised colour. As he watched he thought he saw flashes of lightning within it, although there was no noise of thunder.

He put his hands on the parapet. The bricks were smooth, although the mortar between them had been squeezed out and hardened, as if Guido had been called away before he could smooth it. Nevertheless, the parapet was wide enough to stand on, although there was no rail or barrier to prevent him from falling. Richard took the last few steps up the ladder and hauled himself on to the turret's rim, scared as he did so that the force of his leverage would carry him too far and leave him hanging at the terrifying outer edge.

Once up there he waited for more than a minute until his heart quietened. He did not know if he had taken an irrevocable step and would be too scared to come down. In front of his eyes the bricks were a grey blur.

When he lifted his head he became aware of a light breeze blowing round him. He moved on to his knees as carefully as a man whose every movement is likely to shatter bone. All the time it seemed to him quite probable that he would be seized with vertigo, tumble, and fall to his death. Once on his knees he realised that all he could smell was something neutral and clean, like water, like cloud. And when at last he got to his feet and raised his head, he could see for miles all around – the narrow roads, the villas and farms, the lines of trees, fields of grain, and, not too far away, the lagoon, metallic under the grey cloud. When he looked down at Lucinda's villa the building seemed odd, as if it was one he had never entered; the litter of building equipment, too, appeared unnatural, as if they were components of some irrelevant puzzle.

As he watched, Guido came out of the back door, his hands linked together in front of him. He looked up at Richard, but did not shout.

Richard looked out to sea. The raincloud continued to move away from the lagoon, and a bright line of sunlight was now beginning to cross it, making the water appear incandescent. Richard stood at the edge of the drop and watched. Everything was perfectly silent; he could not hear a sound. And he still did not know why Guido had built the tower.

A COUNTRY PRIEST

THAT YEAR we had the worst winter I had known. It had taken two men with picks to break the ground in the churchyard, and when the soil was lifted it was in great jagged lumps as heavy as stone.

All this was a long time ago. I travelled by horse, although I had once sat in a car owned by my bishop. The villagers told me they never dreamed of owning cars. They were not even sure how they worked, although some of the farmers had tractors. Often, however, the villagers told stories of train rides that would take you to magical places they had never seen – Lublin, Kharkov, Jerusalem. And I would tell them how I had once travelled to cities whose names were mere rumours to them.

That afternoon I took my horse to be shod. It was pleasant to come in out of the street and stand by the blacksmith's hearth. Fire glowed and licked in the bed of charcoal. The smith stood beside his forge, his arms bare and his hair wet with sweat. He was said to be cuckolding one of his friends, but I had seen no proof. I was vaguely jealous of him. At times the life of the flesh, untroubled by the rigours of the spirit, seemed to me to be a strange condition. Like sleep, it was doomed but happy.

The blacksmith's was full of the smell of leather, of pickling fluid, and, most of all, of the hot, sulphurous smell of charcoal. The horse felt the unexpected heat and urinated in a long viscous stream on the flagstones. The smith took its bridle and led it forward. I did not have to say anything; he knew about the shoes by the way it walked. I stood nearer the fire. The horse's winter feed made its urine smell thick and pungent.

The smith bellowed the flames into a glowing, scorching

heat and reshod the horse. As he worked we talked about the village business – the next day's burial, the weather, an expected child. His muscles gleamed as he bent, lifted, hammered. I wondered if hell could be something like this. The smith seemed irredeemably physical. I could see the tension in his body increase and relax, watch the sweat coat his brow. When he rested the shoe or a hammer against his leather apron it gave a soft, almost inaudible thud.

Afterwards the horse backed away, its hooves clattering on the stone and throwing off a few sparks. I took the reins from the smith. 'You owe me nothing for this, Father,' he said, and his smile was thin. I nodded and blessed him. Then I took the horse back across the street and stabled him.

My housekeeper made me a meal of broth and newly baked bread. The bread was pleasant but the vegetables in the broth were fibrous, and some of them tasted slightly rancid. The meat, too, was tough. She was embarrassed by this, but I said it was not her fault, and that I would see if any of my parishioners could give me some better food. Afterwards we drank hot, sweet tea that made me feel heady and content.

The boy came to the door just as I was beginning to doze in front of the fire. I did not recognise him at first. He wanted me to come and see his sister at their farm some distance out in the country. I looked up at my housekeeper and she explained who he was. 'I know,' I said, although I had not known. I was tired and needed rest.

'You must come, Father,' he said, 'I have been told not to come back without you.'

I looked at him, trying to judge from his face how serious the problem was. He repeated his sentence word for word. I sighed, said I was weary, but agreed to come. His face showed neither gratitude nor relief, merely a kind of stupefaction. 'He must be warmed,' my housekeeper said, and made him drink some tea while I got into my boots.

Already the sky was dark enough for the early stars to be seen. I took my horse from the stable and followed the boy on his. Oil lamps burned in several windows, but many had put up shutters. Our shadows were long but already dispersing into dusk. I shivered. The light across the horizon was a narrowing band; it would be another bitter night. I pulled the gloves as tight as I could.

Outside the village all the countryside was frozen snow. Black skeletal trees were dotted around it. Bare thorns lined our track. The sky was darkening all the time, with skeins and clusters of stars springing out across it, and the light wind carried flecks of ice.

Half an hour outside the village we came to the railway. Here, just before they crossed our path, two lines joined. The main line drove straight across the plain, but the branch that came in from the left was from a town that was three hours away by buggy. I went there once a year, twice if I was lucky, and wandered round it. There was a bookshop, and a magistrate's, and shops where they sold things that could only have been brought by train. I always went to the station. It was nearly always empty but, to me, full of promise. It would be an easy place to escape from.

Curiosity overcame me, and I guided the horse beside the lines until we came to the junction. The points were frozen. The spaces between the rails were packed with ice. I went back to where the path crossed. The boy was waiting for me; as soon as he saw me coming he set off again.

But I could not help but pause when I crossed the line. The rails headed somewhere with a precision that was purposeful and thrilling. I never saw them without thinking that someday orders would come from above that would take me out of this bleak, sparse country, away from the claustrophobia of village life. I would catch a train.

By the time we reached the farm the boy had slowed and I was almost at his side. He was doubled forward over his saddle, his head touching the horse's mane. Sometimes he sniffed as if he was crying.

The farm buildings were black and the stonework edged with snow. Outside in the yard stood a drinking trough; its ice had been smashed but had refrozen into a jagged pattern. I sniffed the air and could smell hard earth and the distant fetid smell of cattle. I dismounted and handed the reins to the boy. 'Keep him inside,' I said, 'and give him water and food.' The return journey would be difficult. The boy looked at me. His eyes were full of stars. Then he took the horse across the yard, the ice ridges cracking as they walked.

Before I went into the house I looked around the yard and peered into the buildings. Some hens in a coop fluttered as if I were a prowling fox. And, in an outhouse, there was a tractor that was covered up to wait for the spring. They had money.

I found the pigs by their smell, but I was more surprised to find that they had not had to slaughter most of their cattle for the winter. I slid open the bolt of the byre and went in. The cattle swayed in the dark, their huge black bulks indistinguishable from each other. The place reeked of their warmth, and sodden hay, and shit. I closed the door on them and went into the house knowing I would be rewarded for my journey.

The farmer was thin, with an angular face that exaggerated the slight protruberance of his eyes. He had not shaved for several days. His wife was small and more stockily built, with a broad, open face and a white bonnet that made her eyes look dark and anguished. They fussed around me, thanking me before I even had time to stamp the snow out of my boots.

'How long has she been ill?' I asked.

'She sickened for a short while,' the wife said, 'and fell into a fever this morning.' Her voice was thin with strain.

'She does not know who she is or where she is,' the man said.

'What have you been able to do?'

'We can do nothing but hope,' he said.

'We have prayed,' the woman said, 'All the time we have prayed.'

'Good,' I said absently.

I was looking round the room. It was gloomy but for the fire and an oil lamp in the alcove on the rear wall. Hams, cured by smoke, hung from hooks in the ceiling. The girl's bed had been brought in. It was pushed up against the far wall. I stood in front of the fire and watched her. She appeared to be unconscious; I wondered if she had just died.

The boy came in from the yard, settled himself in a chair, and began to close his eyes. I smiled at him. The farmer took a log from the pile stacked by the hearth and placed it on the fire. The flames licked round it, caught on the resin of the bark, and within half a minute it was spitting, illuminating the room.

I stood next to the girl. She was breathing uneasily and her skin looked sallow and unhealthy. When I touched her brow her eyes shot open and stared at me. She was hot to the touch but my hand, when I lifted it away, was damp. I sniffed it, half afraid of the smell of death.

'Are you a priest?' she asked. Her breath smelled like a dog's.

'I am. Don't you recognise me?'

She looked at me as if she did not understand at all.

'I have known you for some years,' I said.

'Am I dying, Father?'

I averted my eyes. 'I shall sit beside you and pray,' I said.

I would not let them waken the boy, but the farmer and his wife knelt beside me and I spoke a long prayer out loud while the girl lay there. When she turned her head and gave a moan of what I took to be despair I reached out and stroked her hair. It was in damp black strands. Her body gave off a sick heat, as if it was burning itself.

I took hold of her hand and could sense that she had lost much of her weight; the hand was nothing but skin and sinew and bone. I sat there holding it until I began to feel weary. If the girl died, then I would, perhaps, have made her passing easier. But with her presence so close to me, even in her sickness, I could not help but think of her as recovered, healthy, enjoying the pleasures of sensuality with someone I might even know.

I dozed, and imagined that the dark room glittered, as if her soul had escaped her. But then I woke, not knowing how long I had slept.

The girl was breathing more contentedly. I touched her brow again. She was still warm, but the unnatural heat had gone. She could have been a child asleep.

I looked round at the farmer and his wife. He was still on his knees, his hands linked together above his genitals. It was as if he was naked and protecting them. But his wife had her face in her hands. I saw the light run across her fingers then fall with her tears, splashing on the floor. 'I think she is safe,' the man said shakily.

'I believe so,' I said. 'Your wife?'

'She knows that prayer is strong,' he said.

I nodded.

'Did you sleep, Father – or were you entranced?'

I looked sharply at him.

'She believes the Lord was with us. She said she could feel his presence.'

'But you saw nothing?'

He shook his head.

I allowed myself a small, sardonic smile. 'God is everywhere,' I said. But I had never felt his presence. I envied these people neither their ignorance nor their restricted, unalterable lives, but I often wished that God was as real to me as he was to them. For me he was just a theoretical presence, an abstract product of meditation and study, a philosophical ideal.

I put my hand on the woman's shoulder and said some words of comfort. She held on to my hand and kissed it and said how good I was, how I was their saviour, how she had felt God near her and her child. Her husband and I exchanged a glance that neither of us wished to hold.

'You have a rich farm,' I said as I prepared to leave. They began to offer me food, donations to the church, a regular attendance on the Sabbath. I put my fingers to my chin to indicate thoughtfulness and looked at the sides of meat that hung from the hooks in the ceiling. 'We are short of food, my housekeeper and I,' I said, 'it has been a long winter.'

They wrapped the best ham in a cloth and I put it across my saddle when I set off back across the plain. The temperature had sunk still further. The horse's breath plumed in the starlight and on all sides was an unutterable icy silence. The hoofprints that had been made on our journey to the farm had turned glassy and hard. They snapped beneath us.

I looked up at the stars and thought that I had never seen so many. They covered the sky in drifts and clouds of eerie, pure light. They made me shiver.

Out of the corner of my eye, towards the horizon, there was a red flash which scattered and dispersed. Above it the stars were momentarily obscured and then swam back into focus. I was puzzled but not scared. Then the flash again, as if, far away, a smith was bellowing his forge. And the stars above it were veiled and then clear again. I stopped and listened. Far away there was a whisper, like an exhalation of breath.

By the time I reached the crossing the train had stopped at the frozen points. It faced me with its heavy black bulk still hissing. Whatever it carried was stretched away behind it down the branch line.

There was a man at the points carrying a shovel of glowing embers. As I rode slowly towards him he tipped them over the points. The cinders hissed and sparked, filling the air with glowing points of red that winked out one by one. Steam rose from the melting ice.

I paused before the crossing and wondered if I should help him. But, although he looked at me, he did not acknowledge me. I stayed, for the moment, where I was.

He took a hammer and hit the rails. They sang with the blow as it reverberated down the tracks. Then he picked up the shovel again and jammed it down into the gaps between the rails. He scraped and scored until the ice must have given, because he stepped back and signalled to whoever was still in the engine cab.

'Do you want any help?' I called, and my voice disappeared into the night. The furnace of the engine gave a dull, muted roar. The man looked at me then walked over to the large lever that controlled the points. He pushed at it and it swung with a metallic creak, and I heard the tracks move. They scraped across the ice with a tearing, glacial shriek.

The man walked over and stooped to inspect the rails. When he straightened he looked at me again. His face was shadow and pale reflected light.

'The train will pass now?' I called.

Something came across his face that could have been a smile.

'I have not seen that trick before,' I said.

He did not move.

'You must know many things,' I said.

'Perhaps there are some that you could learn, Father,' he said, and as he picked up his things I wondered how he knew I was a priest. He walked back to the cab, threw the shovel and hammer into it, and climbed after them. A spout of steam hissed from a valve and the train began to rumble forward, gathering speed as it came. In awe, I edged the horse forward, as close as it would go.

I thought that perhaps the points squealed as the huge weight crossed them, but now the whole train was clanging and I could not be certain. The engine smelled of grease and heat and distance. Black smoke, livid with sparks, came out of the funnel with a whoosh like emptied lungs. There were two men on the footplate. Red light spilled across them from the firebox, and one was shovelling coal into its furnace. I was not surprised when neither of them looked at me; they had a whole plain, perhaps more, to travel.

After the engine came a long clattering line of cattle trucks. Their tops glittered with frost. The trucks were bolted and had small barred apertures. At first I thought they were empty, but as the first drew level I saw a pair of shocked eyes and a child held up for air. And suddenly an arm was thrust out towards me through the bars, its fingers open. Another arm followed. They would have grabbed me if they could. Beneath the clamour of the train I heard a strange, forlorn cry begin to pass down the trucks. They were all full, and the people in them had been packed as tightly as beasts. I could smell wet hay and excrement. Faces crowded each opening, and hands reached out along the whole train. I would have given them food, or water, or blessing, or forgiveness if I had been able to. But I could never have reached them, and if they had grabbed me they could have pulled me from my saddle, broken my leg and left me here in the middle of nowhere. The train passed me, arms still stretched out, hands spread, like strange white growths opening into the night.

At the very end of the train was a carriage with an open guardrail at the rear. As the carriage drew level with me I saw that a man stood motionless at the rear. He had fierce, black eyes which did not blink, and his face was thin and bearded like an ascetic's. He fixed his gaze on me and it did not waver as the train drew him away. Behind him the cattle truck roofs shone in the starlight.

I watched the train until I could no longer see it, its noise only a distant whisper across the plain. Then I looked up at the stars and breathed out. My breath frosted in front of me; I sensed the turning of the world; everything wheeled and I fell with a dizzying thump on to the frozen snow. The horse snorted and moved away from me as I sat up feeling breathless and weak.

I picked up the parcel from where it had fallen beside me and dashed the snow crystals from my coat. Then, feeling my bladder full, I stood and pissed freely and for a long time on to the ice.

I led the horse across the railway and mounted him at the other side. The tracks were still and silent. Only a faint wisp of steam from the points spoke of the train's passing.

There were still a few lights in the houses when I got back to the village. I saw to the horse and trudged back into my own house feeling faint. Just inside the door I had to kick my boots free of ice.

My housekeeper got out of bed and, wrapped in a thick shawl, put more wood on the fire. After she had put a kettle on she helped me pull off my boots. I held up the parcelled ham and gave it to her when she reached out.

She unrolled it carefully and I saw her eyes glitter when she saw what it was. She weighed it in her hands and the grain on its flank caught the firelight, making her nod appreciatively.

'It's good,' she said, 'it's just what we need.'

'Yes,' I said.

'And the girl?' she asked.

'Don't worry,' I said, 'she was saved.'

The kettle began to knock and hiss. Soon vapour spouted from it. I gazed into the fire until my eyes ached.

ANGELO'S PASSION

'WHAT ARE you reading?'

At first I ignore her.

'I asked what you were reading.'

She walks over to the bed. I try to be still but my instinct is to curl away, protecting the book as if she had nothing to do with it.

'Pliny,' she says, twisting the name with her English tongue.

'Pliny,' I tell her, using the Italian pronunciation. 'You recall that you bought it for me in Venice. In English it would be called *Natural History*.'

'Renaissance?'

'He died in AD 79. You will, of course, know what that year means?' I half expected her to have forgotten.

'Yes,' she says, 'I liked Pompeii.'

Rose is wearing expensive underwear of black lace. There is a subtle, erotic sheen to it. I can think of half a dozen girls straightaway who would look alluring in it. Not Rose. She belongs to the age of white underwear – slips and stockings; the kind of things you see in old films from the fifties and early sixties. After all, this was her time.

She leans over me and places a finger on the text. 'It isn't Latin?'

'I wish I knew enough to read it in the original. It's a translation into modern Italian.'

'*In the middle of the Ptone . . .*'

I translate. '*Among the Ptonebari and the Ptoemphani, upon the coast of Africa, the dog –*'

'Tell me about it.'

So I tell her what I know about Pliny. About his imaginative vision of the world, his bizarre statements, his odd names. How he had taken the bare physical facts of life and transmuted them into the wondrous, the magical, the divine.

She nods. I can see her storing it all in her memory. She'll take away more than just photographs.

There are two books by Rose's side of the bed. One is a colour guide to Italy. It has lots of photographs, all taken in bright sunshine, all with colours that are too intense. Fortunately it does not go into very much detail about the history and culture of the country. For that I am invaluable.

The other is a sex manual. Printed in America but sold in Britain. There are pages of description, references to sexologists and poets, libertines and artists. There are cutaway diagrams, sketches of genitals in various stages of excitement, photographs of couples making love. In one drawing it is as if the lovers have been sliced, neatly and bloodlessly, by a huge blade. All the anatomy of sex is as bare as an opened corpse. There is, it says, no book better.

Rose leans forward again and takes my ear between her teeth. I can feel the pressure, gentle but scary.

'Let me just finish this chapter.'

She sits up and takes the book off me. I give a heavy sigh of exasperation but she takes no notice. 'But it's *pages* long.'

'Really?'

She puts the book face down under the bedside light.

'Bedtime,' she says.

I sink down in the bed. She strips at its foot. The underwear leaves lines across her skin.

Rose plunders the manual. She wants no possibilities left. She wants the subject squeezed dry. So she coaxes, cajoles, shames me into aping its illustrations. She wants to exhaust hedonism. We couple like dogs, with me high above her haunches, hands on her flanks. I dream that she might dry and, like dogs, we will be glued into an absurd, horrifying embrace.

Afterwards she talks her mad fantasies of taking me back

as lover, pet, the envy of all her friends. 'We'll be the talk of Herefordshire,' she laughs, 'Rose and Angelo.'

We both know this will not happen. But we will get value from each other while we can.

I feel tired of it all. I feel bored and disgusted at myself. But I'm too much of a professional to let things go before their time. Rose and I have several weeks together before the end must come.

I allow myself moments of petulance. For Rose, this too is part of my Latin charm. For, just as she loves me to be the smooth talker, the sharp dresser, the cultivated guide, the accomplished lover, so she expects me to be the moody boy, beautiful but selfish, jealous and adolescent. She *imagines* me. And I support her image of me.

But she also imagines herself. She gives herself a race, claiming to be a Celt. Her red hair proves it, she will say, and I think that when she was a young girl it would, indeed, be full red. I have tried to find out more about the Celts from her, but they seem to have left little behind them. I have no interest in barbarians.

In the end, it all comes down to our postures on the bed, and her hissed commands to me, her reiteration of my name.

In the early morning, just as the sun comes up, she finds me in the hotel bathroom. The back of my head is floating on warm water. I feel like an unborn child, only vaguely conscious.

'Are you all right?' she asks, half-asleep but concerned.

I nod.

'Isn't it a strange time to take a bath?'

Drowsy, I merely shake my head.

Only when she has gone back to bed and I have climbed naked from the bath do I realise how badly my shirt has been damaged. Blood has covered one sleeve and spotted the front. I put it in a plastic bag for disposal later. I'll hide it in the car boot and dump it in some roadside waste-bin.

I breakfast on the terrace. Already the sun is warm, and only the faintest of breezes stirs the newspaper. I can hear noises from the kitchen. When the heat has made the hills disappear in haze I put on my dark glasses and hide behind them.

When Rose appears she seems refreshed by the night. She has washed her hair and – I admit it – it looks good. But the lines are deeper at her mouth and eyes, looking as if they are a sculptor's knife incisions on a clay model. And she wears a scarf around her neck. Several times she has caught me looking at her neck and must have noticed some change in my expression. The scarf is red, as bright as blood, but it hides the age that has her by the throat. She would be attractive to an older man.

Like a Caesar, I motion her to sit.

'An interesting edition?'

I grimace.

She leans forward confidentially. 'You were good last night.'

I do not know if I should be irritated or dismissive or proud. I pretend to be proud. 'To be good one must have a good partner,' I say, and hide behind the newspaper.

'But Angelo, you were wonderful.'

I smirk.

The waiter serves her breakfast. He looks at me with that mixture of disgust and envy that I've grown used to over these past few months. And before that, before Rose found me. The waiter thinks he can read our relationship like a book. He would be a fool if he thought that I could not see his jealousy.

'Much news?'

I shrug.

'You look good in that shirt.'

'Thank you.'

'That's the one I bought you in Milan, isn't it?'

'You know it is, Rose.'

'You've changed.'

'You are observant.'

'You change your clothes as often as a woman. That shirt you put on last night was clean.'

'It felt dirty. Even this far north there is still a lot of dust in the air. And possibly this hotel is not as clean as it should be. I must satisfy my vanity.'

'I wouldn't want you any other way.'

I turn the page. The breeze catches it and folds it back.
The waiter moves across the terrace, orange juice held high on a
silver tray. There are the noises of distant radios, the chamber-
maids at work, of washing in the kitchen.

'Are you going to wear your suit to the church? Your
powder-blue one?'

'Yes, I think so. With the sports shoes.'

'The trainers? Angelo, you can't wear trainers with a
suit.'

'Only the very fashionable wear them. I have seen a
photograph of Mick Jagger dressed very like me.'

'Are you sure?'

'There are certain things I do very well. One of them is
dressing fashionably.'

'Of course, lover, of *course*.'

Your lips are too red, I want to say, they make you look
old.

But if I want to keep her I cannot be so direct. I have to go
about things in a round-about way. It is only because of her that I
can travel in this way. She pays for the hired car, the hotels, the
petrol, the food. She paid for my expensive haircut in Florence,
my thirties-style white slacks, the shoes I'll wear if I take her out
tonight. She even bought me the crocodile-skin wallet which I
keep full of her money in my breast pocket.

Yet, in St Peter's she stood before the Pièta and said that
the woman was out of proportion, that if she stood up she'd be
two feet taller than the Christ. I raised my hands in despair. She
looked up at me, almost as if she was scared. 'Tell me,' she
whispered. It was like a panic of deprivation. '*Tell me.*'

So I told her all about Michelangelo and the technical
problem of the seated figure and how it was solved by the basic
pyramidal structure; how, at the end of his life, he did the
Rondanini Pièta, where the form of the dead Christ merges with
that of his mother; how one should look, not for physical
anomalies, but for achievement. For grief and dignity and
passion.

'Passion?'

'In the Biblical sense,' I said, slightly exasperated.

She nodded dumbly, like a child.

'You look,' I said, 'at how the agony is made beautiful. The whole thing is a metaphor for transcendence. That is what it is about.'

So it was during the rest of our extended wandering around the country. I would take her to ruins and panoramas and historical sites; to galleries, piazzas, churches, opera houses. I told her about Ovid, Dante, Leonardo, Verdi, Bernini. I suggested we divert by certain roads, visit less well known places, linger a day or so at small hotels. I would read up beforehand and sometimes have to invent little details, but on the whole I am an honest guide. I have found out a lot of things myself. I'm sure I could make a living out of it.

On the road between Positano and Amalfi she said, 'But this isn't the real south. This is the tourist south.'

'I agree. The north is much more interesting.'

'You don't understand. I want to see the real south. The peasant south.'

'There is nothing there to interest either you or me. There is nothing down there to make any civilised person stop and look.'

'I think we should go. It'll be an experience.'

It was. Its people were suspicious and withdrawn. They disliked people such as us. They thought it was immoral for Rose to keep me. They still believe in darkness and brutality – we saw charm signs on the walls – and they mistrust foreigners. Not even their faces are modern. They belong before the Renaissance.

Rose found them fascinating.

'They are like your Celts,' I sneered, 'with nothing but superstitions to leave behind them.'

I saw them as unexciting but dangerous. She saw nothing sinister in groups of men in dark clothes, their boots covered in dust, standing just looking at us across powder-bright town squares. She thought it was all somehow *real*. 'But these people are nothing,' I said, 'there is no individuality in them. They are the same, generation after generation. There is no reality in them.'

A goat had been tethered outside one of the houses. It grazed a barren circle. One day it was found butchered. It had been degutted; it lay with its head thrown back in the middle of a black riot of flies. Rose was a foreigner; suspicion fell on her. They would not serve us in the shops; they spat after us in the street. They made the sign of the evil-eye when we passed. A policeman, surly and threatening, visited us in our tiny room at the town's solitary hotel. He talked about the fear of witchcraft and said it would no longer be possible to protect us. We left within the hour.

I felt easier when I had put miles between us and the village. 'I hated it there,' I said.

'Why?'

I sought for reasons. 'It's too hot. Too barren. Too near Africa.'

When we stopped I walked around the car and realised that someone had taken a knife along the side.

'All right,' I said, 'Foggia, Pescara, Ancona. I shall feel happier the nearer we are to civilisation.'

Sitting here this morning, reading my copy of *Il Giornale*, digesting my breakfast, I feel a lot more comfortable than I ever did in the south. This is what I was made for, I think, and start to read an article about Venice.

'Are we going to that church this morning?'

'Yes. The frescoes are damaged a little, I think, but still worth looking at. In England you will never have heard of them. Italy is so rich that only a very few things are known about abroad.'

'Angelo, you'll make them come alive for me. You always do.'

'Where shall we go after this? I think it is time we began to move on.'

'But yesterday you said you thought we should stay a few more days. Have you changed your mind?'

'I thought about it overnight. In the bath. There are so many things to see. I want you to have the best of all possible times.'

She leans forward and grips my hand. I give her my special smile. Not for nothing did I have some teeth capped.

'Just let me finish this,' I say, 'and then we will go.' Sooner or later I will pass through Venice again. I need to know what's going on.

From behind me I hear a high, distressed voice. It carries through the sunlit morning with surprising clarity. I know who it is. Ever since we arrived here a fat woman with dyed black hair and a loud reedy voice has insisted on demonstrating the affections of her cat. She carries it around in a wicker travelling-box. She feeds it from her table, talks to it, tells people about its health and habits and intractable sexuality. The waiters, sensing money, humour her. They pretend to be amused by it. They even offer it special food, slices of veal or fish. They are fascinated by it, but it is obvious to me that they hate it. The cat, which is black and furry and groomed, remains sharp-clawed, thought-less, unapproachable. It opens its black jaws to reveal a mouth of moist, glistening pink, and sharp white teeth.

'What's all the noise about?'

'A missing cat.'

'That woman with the pet cat?'

'Someone must hate it. A waiter, perhaps. One can only take so much.'

'What's happened?'

I shrug as if uninterested and raise the paper to cover my mouth. 'It has been killed. Not in an accident, but by someone.'

She looks at me with a steady uncritical gaze. The cat owner's voice subsides into tears. I can hear the sympathetic, lying staff console her. They cluck around her.

'The walk to the church will be lovely,' Rose says.

'Yes,' I say, seeing the lifeless cat placed carefully back in its wicker carrier, its fur spiky with blood.

We don't say much during our walk. The sun is very pleasant, not too hot, and there is little traffic. No one joins us.

The church is pleasant but unexceptional, its importance over-emphasised by the local guide book. But it is quiet and cool and old, empty enough to give hollow reverberating echoes. It is easy to feel part of a less flippant, more accomplished age. I don't like their crucified wooden Christ, which is of too recent a date. It is too disturbingly physical for the quiet seriousness of the church. There seems to be no resurrection hidden within.

'Is this good?' Rose asks.

I pull a face. 'If you like that sort of thing.'

'It reminds me of something I once saw. I think it was in Germany.'

'Protestant Art. There is no glory in it.'

'You see no achievement?'

'I see no spirit.'

We walk round to the frescoes. They show Christ borne by angels in heaven, whilst sinners and unbelievers suffer in hell below. The hell is still in good condition, its torments vivid and bizarre, but mould has crept across the heaven. The angels and the Christ have begun to disappear, like something delicate that has been passed over by a flame.

'But this is terrible.'

'Really?'

I haven't heard her. I feel like reaching across and touching the Christ, as if the hand of a believer will somehow cure this sickness and decay. But I know I would only touch stone and the powdery fungal specks of dead paint.

'Look at this. It's a scandal. Public funds should be given to protect it. It is no masterpiece, but it is *real*. Now all the lightness and sureness has gone. The Christ is almost destroyed. It has a few years. Maybe five, but no more. Perhaps it is already beyond salvation.'

'It must end shortly.'

I smack my hands together. The noise echoes down the church. 'What are we if we cannot look after our own greatness?'

She nods. 'Yes.'

All of a sudden I realise what she's talking about. 'Shortly?' I ask, shocked.

She smiles.

'You mean I'll have to earn my own living?'

Rose walks along the frescoes. 'You've opened my eyes

to things like this. You really have, Angelo. I couldn't ever forget our time together. And I've learned so much. About all sorts of things.'

I follow her down the church, meek as a slaughter-house lamb.

'It's terrible about the paintings. You're right. We have a local church with carvings that are hundreds of years old. Done about the same time as these, I suppose. But we had very different styles.'

'Rose,' I say.

'They're very strange. Offensive, even. Not the kind of thing someone like you would expect in a church. I grew up with them, so I don't have that problem. And they've lasted far better than these poor angels. One is a *sheela-na-gig*. You've heard of such things?'

'Rose.'

'What a pity. It's a very old word. It means a carving of a woman. Holding herself apart. Do you follow me?'

Our footsteps echo in the cool, centuries-old silence.

We spend the night at a hotel two hours drive away. Rose gives me a present. I can tell that it is a thick, heavy book. I wonder if this is as a farewell.

I unwrap it.

'Michelangelo.'

'You like it?'

I open it up. It is beautiful. 'Yes,' I say, 'very much.' I turn the pages. 'It must be one of the best.'

'*The* best.'

I find the Rondanini Pièta. It is photographed from several angles in different kinds of lighting. The forms sink back into the stone, unable to escape. It is as if holiness has escaped even them. They fall back into the world, like animals without souls.

Three days after we part and I have found Elizabeth. Elizabeth has dyed her hair ash-blonde but I can tell what colour it should be by looking at the roots. She is overweight. And she is half-embarrassed by the attention I pay her. But also she is half-excited.

I am a lot younger than she is.

She pretends to try to reject me, but I persist. It is, after all, what she hopes for.

I promise to take her to see the land of Bernini, Dante, Giotto, Tasso, Pliny. Lights of ambition shine in her eyes.

'I'm too old for new ways of doing things,' she tells me later.

'Nonsense,' I say, 'you are a very attractive woman.'

But when we couple like dogs, I sense the same fear that gripped me when I was with Rose. I am trapped by flesh. Dizzy, scared, I finish the operation in a cold sweat and fall on the bed shaking with fear. She does not even notice.

Among the Ptonebari and Ptoemphani of the African coast, the dog is worshipped as king. Priests study and interpret every movement. Each twitch or scratch, each lift of the nose or tilt of the head, each emptying of bladder or bowels, each wag of the tail or closing of the eyes, each sniff or bark is taken as a commandment. Each of these commandments is followed religiously.

FOGGED PLATES

RENFREW WAITED for the Parkers in his dark funeral suit. The grandfather clock ticked heavily in the corner; they'd be here in five minutes, coming down the broad main street with the small coffin, the undertaker meeting them at Renfrew's door.

The suit was tight under the arms. Renfrew liked to leave the jacket loose until the last moment, when he buttoned it to be more in keeping with the sadness of the occasion. He checked in the mirror that his expression was mournful. He'd also draped the corner of the studio in black. Tastefully, he thought. And he'd cleaned his boots, which got covered in dust if he stepped outside. Sometimes, after high winds, the boardwalk outside was heaped with ridges of sandy dust and the inside of his studio invaded by veins of it. It got everywhere. During duststorms he worried constantly about the equipment.

Renfrew opened the door a little and peered through the crack. Outside the sun was hot and nothing much moved, although a tethered horse flicked its tail lazily and stooped over the water trough. On the opposite side of the street a dog lay motionless in the thin shade of an awning.

There was no sign of the Parkers. Renfrew looked in the other direction and saw the undertaker doing the same as him, peering out to see if his custom was arriving. The undertaker's head dived back into his workshop. It was unseemly for them to acknowledge each other beforehand.

Renfrew hoped the Parkers would hurry. Despite all the precautions, they couldn't wait long in weather like this. It would be as well if the job was over with as quickly as possible. Renfrew closed the door and turned back into the studio; to the black drapes, the racks of chemicals on the wall, the boxes of glass plates, the large heavy camera mounted on its tripod in the middle of the room. Last night's events were still in the air. Last night, for the first time in his life, he had photographed a nude.

She'd sneaked in at night. He'd gone around the studio and bolted everything, made it tight as a cell, even put up the outside shutters. He wanted no one to be able to peer in at the narrowest crack. Inside the air was stifling, like an oven, but he'd kept on his working clothes to maintain propriety.

She was a wide-hipped, big-buttocked girl from the brothel down the street. All decorum was observed; she undressed behind a screen. Renfrew, who had his reputation to maintain, had only seen her from a distance. A go-between had arranged the appointment. While she undressed Renfrew talked about Art, and how he would look at her body, not as one of her customers, but as someone interested in Higher Things. He had to speak up because she couldn't hear him over the noises of clothes being removed. And at times she couldn't understand him anyway – his voice had become thicker and he talked more quickly with the excitement of the session.

When he picked up a glass plate his hands shook so much that he dropped it and it broke apart on the floor. 'It's all right,' he said, to calm her, 'there's no harm done.' Then he lied and said, 'It was a fogged one, anyway.'

Renfrew got her to take up different positions and then photographed her in the intense, eye-aching flashes from the magnesium holders he had set about the studio. At each flare her big-boned, statuesque body seemed to dissolve in the light.

He posed her as if she was a Roman maiden, naked but for a flimsy white drape across one arm. As a water-carrier, with a fake amphora hoisted on her shoulders so that her large breasts lifted. As a muse or grace, back to the camera so that she showed strong shoulders and broad thighs, offset by the surprising delicacy of a raised forearm. As a courtesan, stretching herself on a couch he had covered with an old peacock feather and long satin drapes. As a futuristic warrior, half-naked in part-armour, her shoulders and thighs protected but her torso bared. Each time the flare was touched off, the room disappeared into incandescence.

Afterwards she had dressed behind the screen. He had sat beside the exposed plates, feeling weak but exultant. She left, quietly, to resume her work in the brothel.

Now he had moved everything. The jar, the silk, the fake armour were all stocked away in his storeroom. The black drapes had transformed the room from seraglio to mausoleum. Yet, the nude girl's presence was still there, like a taste in the air.

He heard the undertaker walking on the boardwalk outside. The boots made slow, measured footsteps. Behind them, lighter, quicker, more uncertain, were others. The undertaker's boy.

Renfrew went back to the door and opened it. The undertaker was standing there sweating in the hot sun. His face was set in funereal solemnity but the back of his collar was already edged with sweat. He glanced sideways at Renfrew, and indicated by a slight, almost imperceptible nod of the head that he should look down the street.

The Parkers were on their way. They were a poor family who farmed the degraded lands outside of town, so they could not afford the undertaker's best buggy, let alone his two black-plumed geldings. They brought the coffin in on their own cart. One solitary farmhorse was between the shafts. It moved slowly in the heat.

The Parkers walked beside the cart. Beneath her black bonnet Mrs Parker looked as white as chalk. A few strands of hair had escaped from beneath the bonnet and had fallen across her face. She did not push them back. The hem of her dress was covered in dust and she walked with the characteristic lop-sided gait of someone whose broken leg had never properly healed. The eldest girl and idiot boy walked behind her. The girl was silent. The boy had a stick which he repeatedly thrust between the spokes of the cart's wheels. It made a wooden ratchety sound. No one prevented him from doing this.

Mr Parker had the grained, emotionless face of someone who spent his life working unrewarding land. His hat was pulled down so that his eyes were in shadow. After he had hitched the horse he pulled the coffin off the cart. Wood scraped on wood. Across the street a few faces peered out of the dusty windows.

Renfrew held the door open for Mr Parker as he carried the coffin inside. He had it laid across his arms with his hands curling up and clasping one side. It was as if he were carrying a log.

'My sympathies,' Renfrew murmured, stepping aside as the small coffin passed him.

'Where should I put her, Mr Renfrew?' Parker asked. His voice was low and shook a little. It sounded as if he was scared of asking Renfrew the wrong question or doing the wrong thing.

The other Parkers came in and stood looking down at the studio floor. Except the idiot son, who gazed around him with his stick still in his hand. The undertaker sidled in behind him. His boy stood in the doorway with a bucket in his hand.

'Close the door,' the undertaker hissed at him out of the corner of his mouth, in a voice loud enough for everyone to hear. The boy stepped quickly inside and closed the door too loudly.

Parker stood silent, bearing his terrible burden in its wooden box.

'How do you want it, Mr Parker?' Renfrew asked. He didn't know whether to call the child *it* or *her*.

'I think she should be lying in her coffin,' the undertaker said. Renfrew glanced across at him. The undertaker had spoken in a surpisingly firm tone, as if he would be prepared to argue with any other suggestion. At this of all times.

Mr Parker looked at his wife. She nodded.

'Buisiness is business,' the undertaker murmured to Renfrew.

Parker put the coffin down on the floor. It looked absurdly small and made everything seem helpless and bitter.

'Have you a place for the photograph, Mr Renfrew?' asked the undertaker, knowing only too well where Renfrew would photograph the child.

'Mrs Parker?'

She turned to Renfrew. Her face looked numb, as if the distress had shocked her very nerves.

'I can get a better exposure –' Renfrew checked himself. These people would not know what he meant. They were spending some of their hard-earned savings on this record. The least he could do was to make sure they fully understood what was going on. 'I can get a better photograph over there, Mrs Parker. I need good light and we can open the shutters on that side of the studio. It will make the photograph sharper. Clearer.' After a pause, he said, 'The face will show up better.'

She looked confused and glanced at her husband.

'That'll be fine,' Parker said.

Renfrew clapped his hands. 'Good,' he said. He moved over to the far wall of the studio. The shutters had already been opened and merely had to be folded back. The idiot boy followed him. The idiot boy had fine sparse hair and bulbous eyes. His cheeks were sunken like an old man's and his skin was un-naturally white.

'Of course,' Renfrew said, 'we could take the shot with a flare if you wished, but that would be more expensive, and I know how difficult things are for you financially anyway. They're difficult for us all these days, aren't they? It costs me a lot of money just to keep my stock at the right levels –' He started to talk more and more about the need to buy lenses and plates and chemicals. He did this because he was watching the idiot boy eyeing up firstly the camera, then the drapes, then the chemicals at the back of the studio.

'We'll just prop the coffin up here,' Renfrew said, indicating the area of sunlight that now fell across a part of the studio floor. 'That will give me just the right conditions to take the picture.'

The undertaker knelt down beside the coffin, but, before he could do anything, Parker cleared his throat nervously and loudly. They all looked at him.

'Err, Mr Renfrew?'

'Yes?' Renfrew wondered what was coming.

'Have you anything . . . well, another room or some-thing?' He looked round the studio, his eyes darting from corner to corner in a kind of desperation. 'Or that screen maybe?'

'What's the problem, Mr Parker?'

Parker and his wife exchanged anguished glances. The daughter held her hands in front of her and gazed at them. The idiot son tapped his stick on the floor of the studio.

'It's the dress,' Parker said, 'we need the dress.'

Renfrew still didn't understand. But the undertaker did.

'The little girl's in a good dress, Mr Renfrew. Probably belonged to this little girl here when she was smaller.' The daughter turned away pointedly. 'I'm sure Mr and Mrs Parker will have another child, Mr Renfrew. A strong, healthy girl, maybe. Good dresses cost money. And they're difficult to get. Who would want it to lie in a grave?'

Renfrew had realised his error and begun to blush at his own obtuseness. 'Of course,' he said, 'of course.' He pulled the screen out so that it protected a small area in front of a few jars of chemicals. 'After the photographs you can change the little girl behind here. Is that all right?' Only now had he realised that Mrs Parker carried in one hand a small tight bundle of coarse white material. The shroud.

Parker was relieved. 'That's fine, Mr Renfrew. We're really grateful. It just seems more fitting.'

The undertaker took a small, thin lever from the inside of his coat pocket. The assistant stepped forward hesitantly. The coffin lid was held on lightly by a few nails. It came off easily, although part of the wood splintered on the sides of the box. The undertaker made a thin, perplexed noise at the back of his throat and pressed the splinters down to be flush with the wood. Then he lifted the lid fully away and laid it on the floor.

Renfrew looked across at the Parkers. Their expressions hardly altered.

The child lay in the coffin with half-open eyes. Even though the coffin was packed with large, irregularly shaped chunks of ice, her face had the peculiar colour and texture of something beginning to decay. Renfrew shuddered.

The undertaker slipped gloves on his hands and picked the ice out of the coffin piece by piece. The undertaker's boy came and stood by his side. The undertaker put the ice in the bucket, fitting it carefully so that there was maximum contact between the faces. Ice was precious. He wanted to lose as little as possible. When he had finished he nodded to the boy who walked smartly to the door and went out. Renfrew could hear him run along the boardwalk.

'Right, Mr Renfrew,' the undertaker said briskly, 'I think we can get a move on now.'

They carried the small coffin to the sunlight. The girl's dress had been drenched with some kind of cheap perfume. It was rich and cloying. Renfrew carried the head of the coffin so the half-closed eyes would not appear to be looking at him.

While the undertaker wedged the coffin into position Renfrew checked the camera and drew a small crate of glass plates across the floor. But even through the camera lens the dead child looked disturbing, even sinister.

'It's a beautiful dress,' he said, more to fill the silence than for any other reason.

'Yes,' Mr Parker said quietly.

'It's *my* dress,' the other daughter said petulantly.

Mrs Parker made a shushing noise at her.

'I have to make a few exposures –' Renfrew began, then checked himself. 'I have to take a few photographs,' he said, 'two out of three of the glass plates are fogged. You don't get good reproduction. You want a good photograph of the girl, of course. But I'll have to charge you for the number of plates I use. Sorry.'

Mr Parker looked momentarily hunted. But after another glance at his wife he said, 'Two out of three, Mr Renfrew?'

'I thought I'd use four. Just to be on the safe side.'

'Four.'

'As I say, you don't get good reproduction.'

'Four, then.'

Renfrew worked as fast as he could, although he was distracted at one point by the idiot son who came and stood very close to him and looked at him with eyes that were both empty and accusing.

'You needn't worry about the damp on the sides of the dress,' he said, 'it'll show as shadow.' The dress was sodden where the ice had melted into it. 'And I'm sorry about the number of plates.' He began to tell them about the difficulties of supply, but stopped. They were farmers. They knew as well as he did that resources were not renewable. As the undertaker did, when he went to the hill outside of town and dug the sand away from part of the fallen forest so that he could make coffins.

'That should do it, Mr Parker.'

It was a relief to finish. The idot son gazed vacantly at his dead sister.

'Can we change her now, Mr Renfrew?'

'Please.'

The Parkers carried the coffin behind the screen. Renfrew busied himself with the plates, watched by the daughter. He tried to smile weakly at her, but she did not respond. The undertaker, eager to be off, cracked his knuckles.

From behind the screen came the rustle of clothes being removed. Renfrew was reminded again of his nude model. His tongue protruded slightly from his lips. He bit it gently.

Then he heard another sound. Rhythmic, resonant. The noise of a stick being trailed across a long row of jars. His chemicals.

He didn't pause, but ran behind the screen, his mind full of broken glass, spilled liquids and powders, ruin. The idiot had his stick arm extended, but his father had already stopped him playing on the bottles. Parker looked at Renfrew, his hands restraining his son, as motionless as a photograph. Renfrew looked beyond them to the child in the coffin.

Mrs Parker had taken off the dress. The small corpse was propped up so that the shroud could be wrapped around it. It was naked. At the base of the ribcage a strange, wrinkled growth protruded from the body, like a dead fruit – except that Renfrew could see a toothless mouth, closed eyes, slits for nostrils. Mrs Parker pulled the shroud across her daughter's body and hid the head from view. The half-open eyes of the dead girl looked down at Renfrew.

Renfrew turned away and walked across the studio to the undertaker. Despite the heat, he had begun to shiver. The undertaker looked at him as if he had seen it all before.

The Parkers carried the coffin to the cart outside. The same few faces were still at the windows across the street. A hot wind had begun to blow and send thin whirls of sand and dust down the lines of wooden houses. The coffin scraped noisily on the cart.

Renfrew felt ill. He licked his lips but tried to remain composed. The undertaker eyed him as he passed, as if to warn him to control himself. A *strange* birth, he'd told Renfrew, and lingered on the word. But Renfrew hadn't realised.

'Thank you, Mr Renfrew,' Parker said, and extended his hand. 'I'm obliged to you.'

'Call in a few days,' Renfrew said, swallowing hard to make himself sound normal, 'the photograph will be ready by then.'

'I heard that once there were cameras that took hundreds of photographs. That isn't true is it, Mr Renfrew?' He looked up expectantly.

'It's not true.'

'I never knew whether to believe it or not. They say there was a golden age when all those things were possible; people travelled as fast as the wind, everyone was healthy and strong and fruit was always there to pick.'

'I've heard those stories, Mr Parker. Take it from me, it's technically impossible for a camera to take more than one photograph at a time.'

Parker shook his head. 'I never know what to believe. Who are we to know what things were like before Something Happened?'

Renfrew smiled bloodlessly. He knew what was happening to the Parkers. They believed that, long ago, this would not have happened. That somehow they had all been cursed.

'You get lots of mad stories about how things used to be,' he said. 'My advice to you, Mr Parker, is not to believe any of them.'

Parker nodded. The little group set off down the road towards the cemetery at the edge of town. The parents were on either side of the cart, the children behind it. The undertaker led the way. After only a short time it was difficult to see them because the sun illuminated the dust particles in the air.

Renfrew went back inside and sat on the couch. He tried not to think of the Parker child, but he couldn't help it. That one moment of vision was fixed in his mind – the naked child, the parasitic head. A strange birth indeed.

When the undertaker returned he joined Renfrew for a drink in the empty studio. They sat on chairs opposite each other. The undertaker's heavy clothes were damp with sweat.

'There were no problems,' the undertaker said. He was silent for a while and said, 'other than the technical one of keeping the gravesides shored. The soil is too loose and sandy. They say that there are some available soils that are firm, wet. They would hold. No problem.'

Renfrew was thinking of last night's session with the model. Of the tangible statuesque presence of her body.

'She could never have grown,' the undertaker said. 'She was doomed from the start. Those kind of births always are. There are more of them these days than there were when my father was in the business. I could turn your stomach with some tales.'

'I'm sure.' Renfrew desperately wanted to forget the dead child. He did not want her to trouble his dreams. He fixed his mind on the model with a kind of desperation.

'What do you want out of a woman? Someone who can work hard, bear fit children, be your wife and lover and hired hand and support. The girl could never have been any of those things.'

'No.'

The undertaker sat silent for a while. 'In this kind of ground,' he said, 'the bodies get dried out sometimes. Desiccated. The decay gets burned out of them. You come across them when you're digging.' He stared into nothing.

Renfrew thought of his woman. Of how, when he

touched off the flares, her body had dissolved, disappeared into the white incandescence of the flash.

'I have a number of plates to develop,' he said.

They sat there quietly. Sand moved slowly beneath the door, building up a thin ridge of grit across the wooden floor.

'I hope they aren't fogged,' he said.

AMONG THE WOUNDED

I WOKE UP this morning and decided to lie. I did not even bother to reach for the notepad; I just lay there, watching the pale light edge across the ceiling, and trying to forget my dreams. When the nurse came to take off my dressings I saw her glance at the blank page. Her mouth turned down in professional disapproval.

'There weren't any,' I said.

'Doctor will be along in ten minutes,' she said briskly, 'I expect he'll have something to say to you.'

I saw her examine the bandage. 'I haven't bled, have I?'

'No. But perhaps the healing could be faster.'

'You think I'm being cured?'

'Yes,' she said with studied neutrality, 'perhaps.' I wondered how often she had reassured patients who would never get better.

When she had gone I stood up and looked out of the window. Air-conditioning maintains the temperature of the room; the window is locked and I can hear nothing through it. But I can see almost all of the Institute gardens. Already there were one or two patients walking round the grounds, their coats and cloaks wrapped tightly around them to keep out the spring cold. One stood by the far wall, facing the grey brickwork, motionless.

I sat back on the bed and looked round the room. Often I close my eyes and recreate it in my mind, detail by tiny detail. This is not as easy as it sounds, for there are no prominent colours to help the memory. Everything here, from the Scandinavian furniture to the bedsheets, is muted. The books and cassettes have been selected so that they are in delicate, easy shades. There

are no televisions to provide splashes of vividness. Even the
shrubs in the garden have been chosen because their flowers are
almost colourless. Reissmann has told me that the bright
primaries are too aggressive and unsettling, so they are banned. If
it wasn't for the birds I would have begun to forget what strong
colours are. Even then, I have begun to notice that colours remain
in my head like abstract ideals; but when I try to visualise them
they become irresolute and, somehow, puzzling.

When Reissmann came into the room his face was its
usual mask-like calm, but I could tell from his movements that he
was slightly irritated. 'Good morning,' he said. The purr in his
voice was not as strong as it had been.

I smiled weakly and looked back at my hands. Reissmann likes to think of himself as someone whose loyalty and
devotion to medicine are so strong they verge on the ascetic. But
to me the shaven head and steel-rimmed glasses make him look
inhuman, almost reptilian. He scares me.

'There was nothing to write,' I said.

He picked up the empty pad.

'There were none,' I said.

'You give yourself away by defending yourself too
quickly,' he said, and put the pad back down. He sat beside me on
the bed. As usual, his white coat had been crisply ironed. The
dove-grey plastic receiver of a bleeper system was fastened in his
top pocket. 'You must help us to help you,' he said.

'I've been in here too long.'

He sighed. 'You will be in here even longer if you cannot
co-operate.'

'I can walk out any time,' I said, faintly rebellious.

Reissmann said nothing.

'I volunteered to come here. I don't have to do everything you tell me to do. I can go whenever I want.'

'Perhaps,' he said, and smiled thinly.

But I know how difficult it would be to get away. We all
pretend we are free, but we have no access to telephones, the
gates are locked, and we seem to be miles from anywhere. We
never hear any traffic noise other than that of the delivery vans

which unload stores. And it is only by examining their registrations that I can convince myself of the name of the country we are in.

'Can't you remember anything at all?' Reissmann asked.

I shook my head.

'About flying? Falling?'

'Trains going into tunnels?' I sneered.

He clicked his tongue like a disappointed father and I looked away.

'When you were first admitted,' he said gently, 'you were a model patient. You did everything you were asked to do. Now I think you just want to obstruct us. Am I correct?'

I refused to answer.

'It's a common pattern. You needn't think that your reactions are unique.' He paused. 'You're no hero,' he added.

Despite myself, I blushed. I was beginning to think of my refusal as, in its own small way, heroic. He had seen through me.

Reissmann lowered his voice to sound trusting and confidential. 'Everyone who comes here is desperate for help. Terrified, even. Many can't understand what is happening to them, or why. Secretly, of course, you all want to push on. You want to follow the progress of the disease to its limit.'

'Disease?'

'Would it make you feel better if I called it a syndrome?'

I shook my head.

'That's what you must face, you see. The fact that you really do want to go all the way with it.'

'Like Drabble, you mean.'

He tilted his head. His glasses caught the light and screened his eyes from me.

'Are you saying we all want to be like him?'

'Partly. Yes.'

'But Drabble's dead, isn't he? He died yesterday.'

'We don't believe in letting patients dwell on individual cases. I wouldn't concern yourself with Drabble.' Almost as an afterthought, he added, 'Your friend Selma will be able to tell you a little more, no doubt.'

While I was wondering why he had mentioned this, he picked up the notepad again. This time he also picked up the pen which had lain beside it.

'Drabble thought he was safe,' he said, and turned to me with an unblinkingly cold stare. 'Do you?'

He must have seen me weaken. 'Tell me,' he said.

I told him all the details of the dream I could remember. Mostly they were sensations or impressions rather than images – heat, jostle, the smell of sweat and dirty clothes, weight.

'That's interesting,' he said, jotting down one or two words. 'Anything else?'

I shook my head.

'Sure?'

'That's all.'

He tore out the page of notes and put the pad back down beside the bed. 'You know the routine,' he said. 'Tomorrow, as soon as you wake up, make some notes so you're less likely to forget. Dreams are the least tangible part of our work, but in many ways they are the most interesting.'

'But they can't tell you anything. They're meaningless.'

'Your wounds won't go away unless your mind does certain things. Dreams are as good as a thermometer. Tonight I'll bring you something to help you dream. A little present for being good.'

I was seized by anxiety about my own state. I had capitulated within a few minutes; I realised that I was becoming weak.

'How am I?'

'We must continue to work hard,' he said.

I nodded.

'And that means,' he said, 'doing as we are told. Yes?'

'Yes, doctor,' I said.

The meal was, as usual, bland and colourless, but I could detect a faint, gingerish subtlety within it. At first, when I began to detect these odd, disguised tastes, I thought my sense was redefining itself within a narrow range, and that if I had been given the chance to eat everyday food I would have found it to be overpowering, with a sickeningly dizzy range of flavours. Now I have come to believe that what I detect are the traces of drugs I am being given but not told about. I pushed much of the food to one side; even the water had a metallic tang hidden within it.

Afterwards, I went out into the garden. The air was so fresh it made me feel weak, and I had to place each step with the care of someone who thinks he may fall. When I got to the end of the path I sat on one of the wooden benches and looked back across the lawn and shrubs and gravel towards the grey walls and dulled windows of the Institute.

Some of the other patients still walked around the grounds. On the bench on another path the American woman sat crying quietly. She must have been clawing at her dressings, for a bandage lay in limp coils around one ankle. A nurse had come out to help and was kneeling in front of her, binding up the wound.

Another of the inmates, the bearded man who never speaks, walked past and we exchanged glances. Although his face did not alter, his eyes looked wild, almost insane. I thought about how he had first arrived. It had been during winter. The man had been walking a cleared area behind the Institute, but when he saw a robin on the back of one of the benches he went stumbling across the snow, drawn irresistibly to it.

I watched the bearded man walk round and round the grounds. He was like an animal in a pen.

Selma came up to me. Her face was paler than usual, and she seemed short of breath. 'I'm going,' she said.

I looked at her, surprised.

She nodded. 'It's true.'

'When?'

'Tomorrow. I've just found out.'

'You're going home,' I said flatly.

'No – I go to some kind of rehabilitation centre first. Reissmann insists. He says I need time to readjust to the outside world.' She looked across the grounds. An orderly was standing halfway down the path that led towards us. 'They won't want me to reach the outside and say the wrong things,' she continued, 'so they'll be teaching me how to keep my mouth shut.'

'How long?'

She shook her head bitterly. 'I could be there forever.' The orderly took another two steps towards us.

'They wouldn't do that. They just want to make sure you're cured, that's all.'

She held out one hand, palm upward. In its centre was a circular stain of delicate pink. 'I *am* cured, you can see that.' She clenched the hand into a fist. 'Perhaps no one ever really gets out. Unless they do what Drabble did.'

'You saw him?'

She looked sharply at me.

'I thought you must know something. Reissmann said so. I think he must want me to ask you.'

For a while she did not speak. The orderly was pretending to examine a shrub, and had bent over it as if he was a gardener. He was just within earshot.

'For two reasons,' she whispered. 'He wants to know if I will talk, and he wants you to find out what went on. I'm the only patient who saw it.' She put her hands up to her forehead. 'I'm one of his failures.'

It seemed an extraordinary thing to say. I looked round at all the other patients wandering around the grounds. Most of them were sinking into their private worlds. Of us all, it was Selma who had the tenacity to pull through.

'Everything here is organised for success,' she said. 'Your senses are limited so that the physical world loses its edge. We're taken away from family, friends; we withdraw totally. Everything we do has to be officially approved.'

'It helps recovery. They all say that.'

'Then they all lie. They concentrate on weakening your links with normality. I can watch people begin to lose their grip.'

'Like me?'

'I'm sorry.'

But it was true. It should have shocked me, but instead I felt a curiously pleasant resignation. I was content.

'Even the pool is arranged to be part of a desensitisation process. And I don't know what they put in the food. Why aren't your wounds healing more quickly? Do they give us drugs to prevent the blood from clotting?'

The orderly, a slight smile on his face, began to walk towards us.

'And Drabble?' I asked, keeping my voice as low as I could.

Selma stood up. 'I'll say goodbye before I go,' she said, and began to walk away.

The orderly came to stand in front of me. 'Are you well?' he asked in a kindly manner.

I nodded.

He leaned towards me like a confidential friend. 'And did you hear what you wanted to hear?' His eyes were clear and honest.

'No,' I said, 'I didn't.'

'You trust Selma, don't you?'

I hesitated, then nodded. He knew I would believe Selma rather than Reissmann.

'Perhaps she doesn't want to tell you. Should I do what I can to help?'

I was helpless with indecision, but he smiled again, as warmly as any father, and held my shoulder in a friendly, reassuring grip.

'Don't worry; I'll get everything sorted out for you.'

Selma was walking in the back door of the Institute when he caught up with her. I watched them talk for a while, then somehow lost interest and watched a robin fly across the garden, lighting on the backs of benches. It paused near me and looked at me with its bright, blinkless eyes.

After some minutes I realised a figure was watching me from one of the windows. I did not have to look closely. I knew it would be Reissmann.

I used to dislike water. I became nervous with its

lapping, its buoyancy; its closeness to my mouth made me feel breathless. Now I am used to it, and enjoy sliding below the pool's surface into another world. There, all the senses are changed, and there is a feeling of strangeness and ascension. We all do this. Our heads break the surface with water streaming from them. All our immersions are like baptisms.

Selma swims up and bobs beside me. Like everyone else she is naked, but I only notice the way the water makes patterns on her skin, and how, submerged, her hips and legs are dappled and bent by eerie light. Orderlies and nurses are stationed at corners of the pool, standing almost to attention in their white coats. The huge hall echoes with hollow lappings.

Selma says nothing for a while, but she looks closely at me and then around the pool. Everyone else is preoccupied. Some, their mouths only just above the water, are muttering quietly to themselves. Selma takes her feet from the tiled floor and lets herself float, face upward, her head tilted back to maintain buoyancy. I can see all of her body. The small pink blemishes on her hands and feet are the only signs that remain of her condition.

'I leave in an hour,' she says, 'you won't see me again.'

I nod. I have noticed a change in my own attitudes during the rest of the morning, as if I am following some kind of downward curve. For already I have begun to lose interest in her. Life outside the Institution is becoming less and less real the longer I stay here, and today I seem to have sunk deeper within Reissmann's coils.

She pauses, then seems to gather herself for something she does not wish to say but must. 'I was with Drabble in here,' she begins.

I nod. The warmth of the water has a soothing, almost soporific effect. I can feel my own wounds begin to tingle.

'When I saw him I knew he was near to something. His eyes were distant but full of light, as if he had seen something coming towards him from a long way away. He raised his hands out of the water as if he wanted to be lifted up, taken away and saved. The orderlies pulled him out. I remember the water coursing from him as his feet were lifted; I could see the soles, and there was a water-colour stain spreading across from where the wounds were. When they stood him up he was weak-legged, and tottered like someone about to faint.'

I lift my own feet from the floor, feeling the buoyancy take me.

'They took him down the corridor of white tiles. They were partly frog-marching him, partly carrying him. I suppose they must have recognised the signs. I followed them. I wasn't supposed to, you know that. Some of the water droplets on the floor were a delicate pink hue.'

'Yes,' I say.

'I had time to see it start, and then someone grabbed me and took me away. I didn't think blood would come out under such pressure. His scar tissue must have burst open; the blood just sprayed out of him. It covered the tiles.' She is silent for a while before she continues. 'I saw him start to fall. But two nurses were already hauling me back towards the pool.' She gives a sudden, unexpected smile and then looks herself again. 'I remember that my heels squeaked against the tiles as they dragged me away.'

'That was all you saw?'

'Yes.'

'The man died, then?'

'They'll keep the body. I imagine his relatives will never see it.'

'You mean they'll take it apart to try to find out?'

She looks at me with a strange expression, but I dip my head under the water, losing myself in the strange pressures and distortions of this submarine world. When I surface, streaming, she has drifted away. I roll with a lifting swell and let my eyes stray to the echoing ceiling of delicate, faint blue.

Later, when the dull light shows at the corners of the pool, we will climb out and stand together under the showers. Water, soapy and hot, will make our thin flanks steam. We will stand within its benediction, our wounds held up towards its hot and misty downpour.

★

Tonight Reissmann comes to see me in my room. I am in bed, staring upwards, and I hardly notice him when he enters. He shines a light into my eyes, checks my blood pressure and reflexes, takes my pulse. Then he sits back and studies me. 'We asked her to tell you,' he says.

I don't respond.

'We said that if she did, no harm would come to her. And of course, it won't. We thought you would believe her.'

I swallow, absent-mindedly.

He leans forward. 'You would have doubted me if I told you.'

'Yes.'

Reissmann peers at my face as if he is searching for a hidden sign which only he can detect. He puts up a hand and touches my forehead. 'Did she think she would have to stay at the villa for years? She's right, I'm afraid. We don't want such private cases on public show. Besides, matters here are far too important for the public to understand. They would become too . . . emotional.' He takes away his hand, rubs his finger and thumb together as if he is testing something between them, then smiles. 'Don't worry; there's no blood. Not yet.'

I look at him.

He puts his hand in his pocket and draws out a thin, silver-grey case, almost like a pen-case. He sits with it in his hands. 'You remember this morning? I promised to give you something.'

I nod.

'A present. A little something to help you dream.'

He puts the case in my hands. Although its surface is inert, I can sense that it contains something important, and I am almost scared to open it.

He leans closer. 'There's nothing to be afraid of,' he murmurs. I try to put the case on the bedside table, but he prevents me and, instead, folds my hands around it. Then the bleep goes off.

It is a high, regular, rhythmic sound which makes me shiver. For a moment an expression crosses Reissmann's face which could be either shock or pleasure. 'Think about it,' he says hurriedly, and then he walks swiftly to the door. It clicks behind him but I can still hear him sprint down the corridor. The noise of the bleep stops suddenly as he cuts it off.

The light fades across the ceiling.

Still clutching the case, I stand up and go to the window. Outside, in the grounds, shadows fall across the paths.

As I watch, I can see Reismann appear and join a small group which has gathered in the middle of the garden. Doctors, nurses and orderlies are standing in front of a figure in white. There is an odd, ritualistic look to the grouping, as if some drama is being played out. Then a nurse takes one step nearer the figure and falls on her knees in front of it, head bowed. The figure does not move. Cautiously, as if afraid to break a spell, Reissmann walks up to it, one hand raised as if he wants to touch, but is afraid to.

Only then do I recognise Drabble. His face is spotted with blood and there are red patches on his morgue tunic. He reaches out, his hand held high over Reissmann as in a blessing, but then all life seems to leave him and he crumples. The orderlies catch him as he falls.

He is lifeless when they carry him back inside; his eyes are still open but they are glassy, as if he has failed just short of success.

As the room grows darker I go back and lie on the bed.

After a while I open the case. Inside, on a bed of cotton wool, there is a nail made of iron. I take it out and put the case on the table.

The nail has a squat, flattened head, as if it had been struck by a heavy blow. Below the head it is squared, but then tapers to a blunt point. There is a little rust on it; I can sense it on my fingers. This kind of nail was made a long, long time ago, and I can tell by its shape and weight that it must have been designed to hold something heavy in place.

I open my left hand, and press the nailhead against my

palm. After I have done the same with my right, I close my eyes and relax. The nail is clasped in my hands.

Tonight I shall dream of a sun that dazzles, of colour and stench and weight, the thump of wood dragged up steps, the sharp noise of hammerblows, the taste of vinegar. Before my face an anxious bird will flutter, its breast red with lacerations as it tries to pluck the thorns from my brow. Thrilling, mysterious, the side of my body will open into a heart-stopping wound.

When they place my body in the morgue, they will leave the door so that it can be opened from the inside.

BABEL

I HAVE CLEARED a platform on the side of the tower, and shored it with beams and a stone lintel. I keep my belongings, and my fire, just inside its lip; here I can sleep and eat. Further within, beneath the crossbeam, the ropes, the pulleys, is the shaft I am sinking. Already it is many times the length of a man. At first there was nothing but rubble, the infill of walls, shattered plaster with a few traces of paint still clinging to it. Then, by good fortune, there was a natural shaft, a brick-lined emptiness that could have been a flue, a store for water, or a drainage channel. The walls were coated with a grimy damp moss that stuck to the hands like mud. The base of the shaft had been sheared away when part of the tower was forced outwards; I hammered in props to prevent further movement, and laboured for what seemed like weeks among the debris. By the light of a lamp fixed in a niche I had cut in the wall, I sent up stonework, wood, several bucketfuls of broken pottery, the compressed and stinking remains of carpets, several unidentifiable pieces of metal, a tile with a pleasing pattern. Two days ago I heard sharp, cracking noises beneath my feet. I had to lower the lamp to see what was there. Out of the darkness loomed the snapped curves of ribs. It took me a day to dig out the whole skeleton; around its wrist was something made of metal which seemed to have no purpose. But it was untarnished and gleaming, and would be useful to barter at the garden, so I put it among my finds. The skeleton I hauled to the top in bucketloads then tipped it down the slope with the rest of the rubble.

Now I had come to a low, cramped arch. I inspected it carefully with my lamp. The space before was packed with material that could be scooped away quite easily. At my sides and back were huge slabs of unfractured stone; the arch was the only means of progress, and yet I was worried about its strength. When light was held close to it, the stone appeared powdery, fragile, incapable of taking the weight that may rest upon it. If I tapped the arch with my hammer, I could see mortar dust showering through the gloom. The way, I decided, would have to be carefully propped. I struggled back to my shelter, fed several staves through the tunnel, and was by nightfall exhausted and depressed. Before I left the arch, I took a handful of the soft debris which clogged the area in front of it – damp plaster, wood shavings, a leather strap that could have come from a sandal, a piece of fabric which stayed in the shapes into which it was bent.

During the night two robbers came down the tower. A wooden spar, heavy enough to knock a man senseless, came sliding out of the night above my platform, followed by two men with knives and wild, desperate eyes. I was on my feet, crouched with an axe in my hand by the time they were ready to attack. They stood undecided for a few seconds, then turned and went leaping like goats across the black ruins. 'Thieves!' I shouted after them, 'Pirates!' Half a minute or so later I heard a cry, then the clattering of bricks thrown at them from other workings. One of their shadows crossed in front of a fire further down the slope, and then all was silent.

I slept until dawn, then drank rainwater from the cask I kept on my platform. I used a ladle I had found on a previous dig; it gave the water a metallic taste. I stood at the rim of my platform and looked out across the tower. The slopes are crisscrossed by trails, and I could see men move along them, picking their way among the rubble. At times, after heavy rains, the trails disappear and have to be remade through the slippages of masonry, ash, and spoil.

I left the dig to join the main trail. I have even worn my own thin path down to it, for I always place my feet in exactly the same spots. I thread through a litter of splintered columns, and weave my way along the base of a broken rampart. At one point a sapling has rooted, and its thin trunk gives me a precious handhold. Nevertheless, I have considered sawing it down, for if I were to make a find, and am seen taking it to assay, the tree's lone presence on the bare slopes will signal the location of my dig to everyone. On the other hand, were I to be seen sawing it now, others may become suspicious that I have something to hide. It is difficult enough to sleep at night.

The main trail makes its way across a range of buttresses, riven by fault lines, and on to one of the gardens. The garden must be a fraction of its former size, and is canted; at times bricks shower on to it from above. But here the traders grow their vegetables, the nest-robbers sell their birds'-eggs, and, sometimes, you can buy a scrawny chicken. Here, too, is the trading place for provisions and tools brought up from the plains by mule. And it is here that rumour is exchanged.

All of us who live on the tower are at the very edge of survival, and have to pay with our savings or bargain with the trinkets we pull from the ruins. But all the time we hear of those who have made their fortunes, who have tugged out of the debris a silver crown or a golden shield. Always these are at unspecified parts of the tower; always the news is secondhand, blighted by uncertainty, and none of us ever know the man who made the find. Sometimes, though, we become aware that a familiar face is no longer among us. We wonder if he has given up, returned to his wife and family down on the ground; perhaps he is dead within his own workings, a victim of hasty or inadequate propping. Gnawing at us all is the thought that he may have stumbled upon a hoard, made his fortune, gone. We look out over the dim plain and wonder if he is down there, living a life of pleasure and wealth. For we inhabit a place of uncertainty, rumour, unease. Once I saw a man trade a metal anklet for the latest news; whether or not it was true, he would never know.

I walked among the heaps of food, clothing, tools. Each trader has his own language, and yet has adapted to the standardised bartering methods of the tower. All around me people were speaking to each other in low, confidential voices. Someone had seen a whole band of robbers combing the eastern flank; another believed that spirits haunted the ruins, tempting men into impossible tunnels where, trapped, they died slow, lingering deaths; others said that, deep within the conduits, the survivors from the fall still live, driven to incest and cannibalism, and that at night they crawl from their secret entrances to prey upon the diggers. One old man stood at the edge of the trading area, crying like a prophet that the real treasure was neither gold nor silver, but a book whose pages told how the universe was created and would die. That was why the tower was destroyed, he said; to hide the book as if within a secret cave.

Further along, near the precipice of a brick wall, a man sat with his legs splayed out in front of him and his hands held like a supplicant's. 'Once,' he said, 'the whole plain was alive with men, with machines, with quarries, kilns, pits, forges, foundries. At night, as far as the eye could see, there were roads lit by torches. But the tower aspired to the condition of perfection. In Heaven there is an ideal tower, of perfect proportion, design, height, beauty. God could not see his ideal mocked. The tower was razed, the empire fell. That was the end of the golden age. Only its echoes are left, a few faint voices that can still be heard among the ruins. We are left in the darkest of all ages with exhaustion, dissolution, death.'

But the man who sells me bread said to me that this was foolish talk. 'Why,' he said, 'those who have returned to the ground say things are just as they were – nothing has got worse. Things always *were* that way. There is no progress, no decay. The tower was created as it is now, just as limestone is created with the bodies of animals already in it. There was no golden age, no fall. Our memories are as false as whispers in the tower, as meaningless as dreams.'

I picked my way across a section of garden that was studded with decorated stones and came to a man selling oysters. 'All the way up from the plain,' he said, 'a long journey, friend; six days or more. They're worth more than you could pay for them.'

I offered him the metal wristlet; he turned it in the light. 'Well?' I asked.

'If anyone knew what these markings meant . . .' he said.

'You'll be able to trade it down on the plain.'

'Not I, friend. Like you, I have not seen my home for a long time. Like those oysters, this would pass through many hands.'

We haggled for a while; eventually I gave him some more pieces of beaten metal in return for six oysters. 'There are some,' he said, 'who speak of the oyster in their explanations.'

'I know,' I said, weighing them in my hand. 'They say that when the tower was first created there was no gold, no precious things within it. But, just as the oyster secretes a pearl around a speck of grit, so the tower secretes wealth in the darkest parts of its fabric.'

He leaned forward knowingly. 'Do you believe this to be true?'

'Who knows? Perhaps, as we talk, an area of filth is turning into the shape of a tapestry, then into some kitchen appliance – jugs, perhaps, or plates – then into copper or lead or zinc, and finally into silver or gold.'

'Seek out the filthiest tunnels and holes, these men say; for there, in conditions like that of the marsh or the sewer, the greatest treasures will lie. There are even those who prophesy that men, too, are subject to the workings of such a law; that out of some squalid hovel a saviour will arise.'

I held up the last oyster before I put it into my sack. 'You think there will be a pearl in here?'

He smiled without humour. 'If so, then come back here, friend. You will get a fair price for it.'

I clambered back up through the garden and on to the main path. After a few minutes I thought I heard a voice call my name. It is so long since I have heard my name that I had almost forgotten it myself. I stood still, thinking that my senses had begun to betray me. The broken tower rose above me and fell beneath my feet.

I walked on, heard my name again, and turned to see a man clambering after me. He hobbled as if his leg had been injured. Thinking that this was a lunatic, crazed by his ceaseless work within the ruins, I went faster. Also I was scared, fearing sorcery; at such moments one believes in spirits, demons. Smoke from the other digs rolled across the crumbling face of the tower.

The figure followed me up the path to my dig; I could hear the man's footfall, his wheezing. Ready to strike him, I turned with my hammer in my hand. He held up one hand. 'Brother,' he said, 'I did not know it was you. You have become so old.'

I peered closely at the face; it was bearded, lined, dirty.

'Don't be afraid,' he said gently.

I lowered the hammer. 'Your workings?'

'Shored, disguised; I will be back before nightfall.'

I took him into my dig. I still had some bread from the previous day. It was hard, and difficult to chew, but I cut it with my knife and we dipped it in water to soften it. 'How many years have we been here?' I asked. 'Ten?'

'Twenty,' he said, then, after a few seconds, added, 'At least.'

I shook my head. 'You're wrong.'

He nodded slowly, as if it made little difference.

'Our wives and children,' I said, and the words faded as I spoke.

'A week's journey away, if they are there at all. What man could leave his workings for that long?'

It was true. Even if our seam was exhausted, we would immediately start another.

I counted out the oysters – three each. 'I ate oysters on the night before we left,' I said. 'I showed my young son how to prise them open with a blade, how to sever the muscle, how to tip the flesh into the mouth. He was all the world to me then. Now I cannot think how old he will be, or what he will look like. I do not know if he is alive.'

'Or, like us, scavenging,' my brother said, and raised a half-shell to his lips. Juice ran down his chin and he wiped it with the back of his hand. 'You have heard that some compare this place to the oyster.'

'I have heard so many things I do not know what to believe. Some say that the tower is what it is merely to provide a symbol, a story that will live in the minds of a thousand generations. To what purpose I do not know.'

'Yes – and there are those who believe that the tower constantly recreates itself, and that deep within its heart there is a furnace which produces wood, metal, stone, all the bits and pieces of material that a man may find here. Some argue that the coming into existence of shaped wood, worked metal, inscribed stone is irrefutable proof of the existence of God. If we had time, brother, if we had the vision, then we would see the tower slowly recreate itself. In a generation's time, perhaps more, castellated battlements will have formed here, passageways cleared themselves, walls will have unbuckled, buttresses re-formed. The tower will break out of this present condition like a butterfly from a chrysalis. And perhaps, in a thousand years time, the tower will fall again.'

'And the dead within it?'

'Who knows? Listen to their whisperings within your dig, if you can, but you will learn nothing. Better by far just to watch the fires at night, when the whole black side of the tower resembles a sky lit by stars, and one can feel the universe move all around.'

I finished my oysters and laid the empty shells in a small heap at my feet. As in a mirror image, my brother did the same. 'Perhaps it does not even make sense to ask such questions,' I said.

He nodded pensively. 'We do not dig merely for riches. We dig to find out what put us here, and why. To solve the riddle of the tower is to solve the mystery of our own lives. All around us, the theories clash, confuse, and none of us know where to turn.'

We sat in silence for a while.

'I must go back,' he said.

'Yes.'

We had little else to say to each other, and parted without making any agreement to meet again. I watched him as he limped back the way he had come. He did not turn to wave.

When he had vanished I noticed that, opposite my

mound of shells, there were three whole oysters, unopened. Until that moment I had thought my brother was alive.

I made my way back down the tunnel to the arch. I pushed the stones with my hammer to see if anything moved, then cleared a space among the detritus. As soft as dried peat, it came away in wedges, tiny pieces of metal glinting in the dark surfaces. All the time I tried not to think of my brother.

I hammered the props into the arch with a kind of angry precision. The sound of the blows was sharp, and yet it choked within the confined space. Satisfied at last, I dug my way beneath the arch, the headspace narrowing until I was on all fours. The peaty substance was scattered across the floor, and above me was a large seamless slab. I held the lamp up to it and saw that it was as smooth as if it had been worked upon by a master mason.

Wriggling now, I pressed ahead, the space tightening around me until I was breathing in my own breath. All around me I could sense, in the blackness, the terrible weight and mystery of the tower. Then, at last, I came to a stop.

Here, wedged into a tiny space, I felt ahead with my fingers and found great unbreakable slabs of stone, with only the tiniest of gaps between them, as if they had been forced apart infinitesimally.

It was here, unable to go forward or sideways, that I began to hear the voices. Dry as leaves moving across a stone floor, they rustled through the tunnels and crevices in the rock. There were men's voices, women's, children's; I could hear them clearly, and yet could not understand the languages that they spoke. Always approaching me, yet never arriving, they whispered down the thin spaces; always I thought that I would grasp something – a phrase, perhaps even just a word – but I could not. They did not cease, did not move away, but went on all around me, an eerie whispering chorus that resisted all understanding.

I lay silently in the dark until the lamp went out.

DEALING IN FICTIONS

(a)

LIFE ALWAYS leaves you unfinished.

The love affair that is over and cannot die, the major work that becomes increasingly more complex and expansive but will not stop, the problems of living from day to day that may be remoulded but remain beyond solution – all these resist an end. Their existence continues. Art can be written off, disposed of, forgotten. In life the blade never truly falls.

So Peter felt as the wife he had deserted moved beneath him.

They made love with the intensity of those who have something to prove to the other, and it left them gasping. It lifted them and it dumped them. As their hearts and lungs eased they began again to hear the city noises coming in through the open window – traffic, faraway radios, construction work on high buildings. The curtains let in the sun and moved in the roof-high breeze.

Ruth's book lay beside the bed. Its pages turned.

The breeze paused, the pages rested, and Peter looked at paired images that after a few seconds he realised belonged to a diptych. That geometrical burst of discolouration at the inner edge of each image, like a stylised explosion or star, was the hinge. A glowing Christ, his face suffused by joy and his forehead bloody with thorns, terrified and humbled an everyday family with his splendour. Elsewhere, lovers entered their earthly bliss unaware that a skeleton enclosed them with its scythe. At the opposite side a saint ascended to heaven carried by angels with the wings of swans but the faces of children. Beneath them, in the sulphurous caverns of hell, devils tortured the sinful for ever under the eyes of extravagant beasts.

The breeze lifted again.

Such blends of the erotic and the macabre, of real worlds and the fantastic, gave Peter little insight or pleasure. The wind blurred the pages. They toppled with a whirr like passing wings. Ruth reached over him and closed it.

He must have dozed off for about ten minutes, because the next thing was that he was in bed on his own and a voice was coming from the other room.

She had switched on the radio cassette and was recording a talk by a man with exact tones who used long words and jargon like *post-structuralism, ontology* and *genre differentiation*. 'Heavy stuff,' Peter said, sitting down.

'I'm interested,' she said.

'I know.'

'He died a couple of days ago. The man he's talking about.'

'Who?'

'Zurawski. He was a Polish literary critic and . . . well, cultural analyst, I suppose you'd call him.'

'You always amazed me with the amount you knew,' he said softly.

'You always said it was misplaced knowledge,' she said.

Later there was music. They sat and drank coffee. An ambulance careered down the road outside with its horn high and penetrating.

'Still given up smoking?' she asked.

'I try. What about you? Twenty a day?'

She shook her head. 'Rather more. My luxury. Or my vice.'

'A common enough symptom, I suppose.'

It was as if she had something to launch from. 'Ah,' she said, 'we have symptoms now. Marriage breakup as a medical condition. With symptoms, progression and, by inference, cure. I think of it much more destructively. Like an execution or an explosion. Someone just cuts your life in half. Like the condemned prisoner, I was eating hearty breakfasts to the last.'

'I didn't mean you to take me so literally. In fact I didn't even want you to start talking about it.'

'We can hardly ignore it.'

'We ignored it just now. When we were together.'

'I didn't mean that to happen.'

'You think I planned it?' He had, of course, planned it. 'Some things just happen.'

'That's a slack, glib way of avoiding responsibility.'

Peter got up and looked out of the window. London stretched away on all sides, modulating towards colourlessness with distance. The streets below were coloured stone, cement, rooftiles. And it was difficult to believe that all those people down there had nothing in common but accidents of location. That his marriage to Ruth and his subsequent affair were the result of chance encounters, nothing more.

'All right,' he said, and stopped. Despite himself, and despite all of Ruth's alterations to it, the flat was beginning to be familiar again. The furniture, the poster in the kitchen, the shelf of ageing paperbacks in the corner, the worn carpet – they were all his. He belonged with them.

'I can't stop thinking of this as my home,' he said weakly.

Ruth pursed her lips.

'Well?'

'Well what?'

'Can't you say anything? Anything at all?'

'I can probably say lots of things very badly. I haven't been able to sharpen my phraseology for a while now. Unlike you.'

'That's *over* with, for Christ's sake. How many more times do I have to say it?'

'Oh, I could practise some telling phrases on Louisa, but she *is* a little young. I don't think she'd appreciate it. It would probably make her very disturbed.'

'You always knew how to rub salt into a wound.'

They each said nothing for a while.

'I didn't come round here planning for us to go to bed, or anything like that,' Peter said.

He sat and fixed his eyes on something. It was a painting Louisa must have brought home from school. She would be there now running round the yard with all the other kids, giggling and enjoying the sunshine. He supposed that her teacher had asked them all to paint their families. He was gratified and guilty that he was on it. At least he supposed that; there were three bulbous heads with great wounds of paint for the features. He was sure one would be him.

'Something happened that forced us apart,' he said wearily. 'It was all my fault. I admit that. I was stupid and immature and all that sort of stuff. Just think of me as being ill for a while. That's all.'

She was silent, then asked quietly, 'Does this feel like home?'

He nodded.

'Sorry,' he said, paused, and asked, 'And you?'

'I don't know my own thoughts,' she said.

'Give it a try, go on.'

She put her forehead against the back of her wrist. 'One day I want you back. I think I feel that way now. It's easy to believe that my natural position in life is as your wife and Louisa's mother. Fixed in place, with all the possessions, all the assumptions and benefits that go with it. There's a certain comfort in that. But the next day I'm happy with myself as I am now. I enjoy sleeping on my own. Doing what I want to do. Looking after Louisa without having to discuss what I'm going to do or how she feels and having you disagree about it. It just seems to be an opportunity I should make the most of while I can.'

'I know what you mean.'

'Do you?'

'Don't think you have a prerogative on uncertainty.'

'We were certain once. Or pretended we were.'

He sighed. 'Ah,' he said, 'pretence. Which of us knows the other?'

'That's it, you see. You make a slight joke out of it all. Say *Ah, pretence* in that rather stagey way and hope to defuse the problem.'

Peter swept the floor with an exaggerated bow. She looked at him as a teacher looks at a foolish child. He coloured slightly.

'I don't know,' she said, resigned, 'maybe it's something to do with leaving one's youth behind. Only when you're young is it possible to believe in an ideal with an intensity and a grasp that changes your whole life. You can believe in politics so much that you think the millennium is just around the corner, out in the street, through the window. You can fall in love so deeply that you realise how grand the senses are. You realise exactly what the poets say, exactly what all the songs mean. And then as you grow and mature you think how absurd it all was, how green and trusting you were. And you vow you'll never let it happen again. And it's not that you won't let it. You've moved on. It's impossible now. It *can't* happen again.'

'I really didn't want things to get this heavy, Ruth,' he said, but she had entered the broad stream of confession and was carried along by it.

She told him how she had always had doubts. Well, since Louisa was born. How their arguments, their periods of sullen silence and their apparent need to destroy each other had at last forced her to think of a life without any permanent relationship. How she had believed as a girl that what she felt for Peter was a transcendence available to all lovers.

'It happens to us all,' he said, trying to comfort her. 'We just have to get ahead with compromise, defeat, adjustments, rejections. We learn to get on with people we swore we'd like to kill. We live with each other when –'

'But there's nothing to hang on to,' she said. 'Nothing to fix the sights on. It's not like this table. I can measure this table. I know what it's used for. I can describe it in terms of shape, height, colour, style. It has an objective, verifiable existence, not only for me but for you. We know it's *there*.' She slapped it with the flat of her hand and the sudden noise sounded like a pistol shot in the close confines of the flat. Peter winced.

'With us it's different, Peter. We're not sure what we ourselves feel. Every time I make a statement I believe to be true a little doubt creeps in. I begin to qualify it in my mind. How can I expect to give you anything fixed, objective, dependable? How can you know I'm not just stringing you along, or acting up to what I think are your preconceptions, or lying to myself? The possibilities are endless. There are no certainties. There is no great, unifying understanding, no common ground of belief. We deal in fictions.'

He listened to the street noise.

'But that's all we have to go on,' he said.

'Even my feelings towards Louisa are . . . ambivalent. Does that shock you? I don't know if she shackles me or frees me.'

She talked about their daughter. They remembered her as a baby, how she learned to walk, her first words, the sleepless nights they had shared. Peter began to feel the sharp but sick experience of guilt. It was confirmation that he was needed, no matter how often he was told that he wasn't. The things they had in common were stronger and more important than that which divided them.

'Things pass,' he said, 'but nothing ever ends. It's true. There should be some law of existence that states that. Nothing is ever really finished.'

'I don't –'

He held his hand up to silence her and was surprised when she obeyed. 'It's the opposite side of the coin,' he said. 'So we can't live with the intensity you're talking about, but on the other hand no one crosses us off for ever.' Suddenly inspired into a dangerous act, he got down on his knees and spread his arms like a priest inviting God. 'After we're dead we'll still be here. Every time someone sings the songs we used to sing, every time this flat is occupied, every moment of Louisa's life and the lives of Louisa's children –'

She put a finger on his lips. 'Enough,' she said. She had enough to worry about without a wash of romantic mysticism.

And it was true that as he walked back through the sunshine he began to think that he had flirted outrageously with the realities of their lives. Ruth had been right.

And yet he also thought that maybe they'd be given another chance. Some deity had seen the pattern and arranged for it to be symmetrical.

The more he considered this the less certain he was about it.

He didn't want to think about it.

The leaves were new on the trees, the girls were out in their summer dresses; it was a good day. He stopped in a park to hear a military band play the familiar largo from 'New World' and, as usual, it made him feel that mankind really was a whole. After they'd finished he followed them into a nearby pub. The pub was dark and cool, the wood was polished and the carpet clean. On the way in he almost fell over a Labrador dog which had stretched out beside the bar. Its owner apologised, and he and Peter began a casually pleasant discussion about sport.

He had taken about two drinks from his pint. The man was not reckoning much to Liverpool's chances this year when Peter was distracted, he didn't know why, by something at his other side. He turned. The pub was normal. Then he looked down and saw, standing beside him, a child who smiled up at him.

Something was wrong. He knew it.

The room exploded.

Peter was one of the three civilians who were killed in the blast along with five bandsmen. A six-inch nail hit the side of his head with the force of a crossbow bolt. He was hurled sideways out of the window and on to the pavement outside.

If Tony had been there he would not have been horrified. If God had allowed him to walk unscathed through the blast, to study its effects with a casually divine presence, he would have felt neither sickened nor guilty. If he could have studied it in slow motion like an analyst can study a film, frame by frame, he would have found a panoply of effects. A kind of balletic beauty. Justice.

Of course he couldn't be there. They'd planted the bomb and had to be away, although even at the distance of a couple of streets the explosion stopped everything.

But he'd rehearsed the effect of the bomb in his mind. In

his imagination he watched the casing rupture in incandescent flame, the windows shatter away from the blast in shards and flying crystalline powder, the chairs and bottles and soldiers blow apart, the building collapse.

He went miles out of his way. When he got to the flat Mary was already there, waiting for him. 'Thank Christ you're back,' she said.

'Touble?'

She shook her head.

'Nor me. It was like falling off a log.'

She was watching television for the news flashes and had the remote control unit in her hand. She flicked from channel to channel. He sat down beside her and she squeezed his hand.

'A few dead,' she said, 'several injured. They don't know how many yet. We just blew the place to bits.'

They watched the coverage as the images lurched and closed in on rubble, ambulances, stretchers with bodies covered by blankets. If they opened the window of the flat they could hear the sirens wail.

Absent-mindedly he played with a strand of her hair as they watched. 'Jesus,' he said after a while, 'we've hit the bastards hard.'

'You smell,' she said.

'As soon as I got away I started sweating like a pig. I was all right until then. When we were doing it I was calm.' He looked appealingly at her. 'You would testify to that, wouldn't you? You'd swear to it?'

'Of course I would.'

She bathed him. His body looked thin and spare in the wide bath, and the water made his beard wispy and his hair bedraggled. She was struck again by how white his body was, how small the hands were. When he closed his eyes drops of water lay on the lids and he looked like a dead man.

'It was perfect,' she said.

'They all thought things had gone quiet,' he said. His voice echoed like a ghost's. 'Ambulances, police cars, fire engines – they've no idea what to do. We've disrupted everything.'

She put a hand through his wet hair, and could feel the skull beneath the skin. When he opened his eyes and looked at her they were innocent and blue. She kissed him.

'Time you were out. The water's getting cold. It'll do you no good.'

'You're just like an Irish mother.'

'You're just like a fucking English aristocrat.'

He laughed and got out of the bath, walking round the flat with a large towel wrapped round his body as he dried himself. His hair, uncombed, stuck out in all directions.

'It was all so *easy*,' Tony said, 'that's what I can't get over.'

'The next one will be nothing like as simple.'

'We'll handle the next one as easily as we handled this one. No – better. We'll be more experienced.'

'Time for a drink.'

'Christ, yes.'

She came from the kitchen with two glasses and a bottle. He tapped the bottle lightly with one fingernail. 'Symbol of bourgeois decadence,' he said.

She clung to him as he poured the champagne. 'It's too good for the bourgeoisie,' she said.

They clinked glasses.

The champagne made them warm and expansive. Tony stretched and yawned. He was close to rapture.

'I kept thinking,' Mary said, 'what if . . .'

'There are no *what if*s. It had to be done. We did it. If it hadn't been us it would have been someone else.'

'I sometimes think of them as your people.'

'In your moments of weakness? For God's sake, you know how you've changed me.'

She smiled, they grinned, giggled, and before long, triggered by the absurd success of their mission and the sense of euphoric freedom they enjoyed, they were almost hysterical with laughter, hanging on to each other and gasping. The television continued to show rubble and carnage. They took a couple of minutes to calm down.

'You know what this makes me feel?' Mary asked.

When they made love it was with a ferocious harmony. When they had finished they did not know what time it was so they wandered back to the television. All the familiar programmes had vanished, displaced by the urgency of today's news. They had spent weeks watching anything and everything from children's programmes to the Open University. Occasionally they tired of the set and read magazines instead. Tony had tried to interest Mary in the breakdown of feudalism but she had remained obstinately concerned with the practical and contemporary. Without her they could never have done it.

When a policeman came on the screen and remarked that the bombers must be barbarians she said, 'No, surgeons,' softly to herself.

'Jesus,' he said, 'I love you.'

During the night they awoke to hear the sound of huge, beating wings compressing and relaxing the air, but they hung on to each other knowing it was a dream.

The next day they made sorties outside to buy the Sunday papers. Back inside the flat they examined all they could on the effects of the bomb and the speculation as to who they were and what their motives were. And they read about everything else that had happened that day, that week. They wanted to remember their time in all its local and international perspectives. Thus they read not only about Peter (an unimportant person, they thought, without any place in the grand scheme of things), but also about suggested changes in government monetary policy, a royal visit, a tug-of-love child, the problems caused by poorly fitting shoes, and the death in Lodz of an obscure Polish literary critic and historian called Zurawski.

They did not know they were already being watched.

Once the central framework is constructed the idea can be extended in any direction. Additions can be made, qualifications entered, further examples detailed. Perhaps this is why the work remains incomplete. Over the years the author saw it grow like coral encrusting his basic idea. Each seemingly disparate article, each textual exegesis or notation was to become part of the great scheme. And, whatever the weight of evidence, the main crux of his argument would still be seen.

The table faces a large sashed window which lets in sunlight and fresh air. My working papers are spread across the desk. These are sheets of lined A4 paper covered in balloons and squiggles and boxes that show provisional translations and those that I'm happier with.

Three books also lie on the desk. One is a thesaurus, one a Polish–English dictionary. The third is Zurawski's book.

He called it *A Theory of Genre Structures*. I wanted to retitle it, but my publisher will have none of that. He favours such weighty titles.

I'm on schedule, more or less. I can allow myself some time off to read the papers or watch the small portable TV I've installed in the corner of the room. In the opposite corner there is a bed. Sometimes R comes round and we make love. I find this less satisfying than our discussions about culture and the contribution to it of sustained critical intelligence.

Zurawski's plan was to divide the book into two parts. The first is called *Fiction As History*. In this part he examines narrative structures, testing them for comprehensiveness, symbolism, exclusion, naturalism and realism. Possibly he meant to extend the list further, but those he dealt with are:

— the intersecting biographies scheme
— the work of individual growth and development, or *bildungsroman*
— the family saga, or conflict between generations
— the thriller, or work of pursuit – or revenge – and detection
— the comedy, or grotesque, or farce
— the fantasy, or science fiction, or modern satire
— magic realism, or, in Zurawski's phrase, surreal naturalism
— the love story or romance

R believes that Zurawsi oversimplifies things, that his scheme has the feel of something imposed rather than organic. I reply that this misses the point. In providing us with a grid and references, Zurawski has enabled us to take sightings on the processes of evaluation and change.

For Zurawski is not interested in individual psychology or fate, but in a kind of total history, or historic totality. All these genres and sub-genres are approaches, tangents, slices into a totality which any given work (or body of work) can only approximate. We read a completeness into it just as we read the complete body from a biopsy.

The amount of approaches is, of course, infinite. Like some Platonic ideal, the totality always lies outside the grasp. All we can deal with are approximations.

The corollary to all this massive effort of tabulation, codification and analysis was to be Part Two of his work. But he never wrote it. Perhaps he died just before he was about to begin. His potential was suddenly and pointlessly expunged.

All we have is the title, *History as Fiction*, and a few subject headings – *ideology and development, morality and outlook, terrorism and justice*.

Sometimes R and I play guessing games as to how this second part would have been constructed. 'I think,' I say to her, 'that he would have used abstractions as the baseline for his arguments. Turned the argument of the first part on its head, so to speak.'

'What, and moved from generalisations to the particular?'

'I think so. He wanted to show how the only way in which the world can be interpreted is in a fictional sense. That one's beliefs, religion, politics are no more *real* than, say, Leopold Bloom, or Hamlet, or Tarzan. That there is, in the world, no such thing as the verifiable – not when you're talking about life, and how to live your life, and what people think are great universal truths.'

'But how can you say that? If there is no evidence to enable us to grasp any truth, if all we have to go on are approximations, then aren't you providing your own great truth from the limited evidence of what he left behind him? Isn't such a thing in itself a fiction?'

I consider this.

'Yes,' I say, 'I suppose so. But it's the only way I can get to the whole. Art always tends towards completeness, no matter how limited it may appear. There's no such thing, in art, as a completely pointless death. Everything has a purpose.'

'Ah, that's the distinction. In art, meaning stalks everything.'

'Just as we make it stalk the parts of our lives that surround us. They may be random, accidental, the results of chance alone. But we lead meaning sniffing around them like a pet Labrador, hoping it'll find the pattern.'

I sit and brood about the impossibility of the task. The wind stirs my papers, turning them, making leaf topple over on to leaf. They whirr with a steady beat, like passing wings.

I cannot decide if, hidden within Zurawski's work, there is the idea of a solution.

(b)

It was Ruth who identified Peter. She felt that nothing in her life had prepared her for this. The Warwickshire childhood, the years at university, her first unhappy affair – nothing had made her expect this.

He was stored in a pullout freezer cabinet with a tight white bandage wrapped round his head and chin. He looked not dead but drugged, as if he was awaiting an operation rather than cremation. But he was dead all right. The temperature of the skin jolted her like a shock.

The bomb was there by careful design. Peter's presence was an accident, a freak of location. That was all.

Even though she kept thinking *if only*, she knew she

could not live her life in a thicket of possibilities that never happened. She determined to live it in as positive a way as she could.

She succeeded.

Many years later, the owner of her own small business, the mother of a teenage daughter, the wife of a dapper administrator in the arts, she was to attend an exhibition of the work of Belfast children. The paintings showed soldiers, armoured cars, gunmen, barricades. In one a man and woman fled from a stylised explosion which tossed arms, legs, bodies into the air. The bodies were featureless but the bombers had the flat, placid faces of icons.

(c)

If this spanned generations, then a part of it, a few chapters perhaps, would tell how one of the family sons rebelled. How his parents, themselves the product of toil and secret business deals and social climbing and affairs, cut him off as he disappeared into a seedy world of bedsits, arms deals, revolutionary plots. How he turned his back on wealth, and society parties, and the Range Rover set, and entered the underground.

He met a girl from a family of poor Irish farmers drawn into the rundown terraces of the big cities. Her zeal, her fervour had a grandeur about them. Her family were sympathetic, but too cautious for action. She heard tales from her grandfather, a boy soldier who'd killed a Black and Tan with a pistol. Her parents begged her not to be so rash; things would sort themselves out in time.

After they died, the families continued. There were other sons, other daughters, another generation. Life carried on.

(d)

Our detective must be honest. Compromised, less than successful, but incorruptible. He'll have a sharp wife with whom he maintains a dull marriage. She'll be a *cordon bleu* cook or a terribly bad one, I haven't decided yet. But she'll know she is secondary to his job.

Since he is British, he cannot afford to have a sharp, romantic and toughly American name. His will be an idiosyncratic name, the name of a rundown seaside town or a shabby piece of clothing.

The breaks, when they come his way, will be part intuition and part sheer, unrelenting, footslogging work.

And he'll fail in so far as they'll plant the bomb just a few days before he can get at them.

As regards the terrorists, the thriller must maintain a factual exactness. Their beliefs will be underpinned by theoretical and historical references. The careful reader will draw correspondences between these and the detective's confused but morally superior liberalism.

Most of all it must be exact to the point of treason on the mechanics of a terror campaign, the black market in weapons, the economic support for terrorist groups. It will even tell you how to make a bomb.

The detective will not want them dead, but they will be killed. Shot down in cold blood on orders from above. When he argues furiously against his superiors, he finds a nest of compromise, appeasement, and moral weakness.

He alone does not have ambition.

(e)

Ruth never confessed she had a lover with whom she

indulged in active bouts of sex. They yelped and rolled across floors, more like animals than humans, knocking their heads against chairlegs. They covered up their affair with ludicrously convoluted arrangements and alibis which Peter was too dim to see through.

The Labrador in the pub was disembowelled by the blast. Its body came to rest upside-down, legs apart, on top of the video game in the corner.

When she identified Peter she smelt a clinging, fetid odour that she thought must be something to do with bodily preservation or decay. It was, in fact, the mortuary attendant. He'd been unable to resist breaking wind just before she walked in. Now, almost doubled up, with pained expressions flitting across his face, he teetered on tiptoe at the edge of her vision, filled up with explosive gases and holding them in by a supreme effort of the sphincter.

The final raid was a chaos of misheard instructions, mistaken identities, wrong conclusions. Policemen tripped over each other in a silent Keystone flurry of limbs.

What other cliché would you like? A stoned-drunk customer, bottle in hand, to stand among the wreckage and to say 'My God, that was strong stuff'? A selfish, boorish and violent man, who had just denied the existence of God, to have his hands fixed by nails to the wall like Christ?

(f)

Peter was transported to an alternative universe where he fought dark creatures of the imagination, monsters from the id, with scales of fur and tongues of fire. His only help was a trusty Labrador dog, transported with him to the same mad world.

Or, alternatively –

Peter was transported to a parallel world where, history having taken a different course, he became a Gulliver in a distorted, fragmented, mirror-image of the world he had left.

He could go into a multiplicity of universes, and in some of these the explosion would never have happened. Because it had no cause to happen.

(g)

He stood in the pub with a drink in his hand. Heard a noise and turned to one side. Standing beside him a child with its face bathed in light. Around him the room blows slowly away, ripping away like burned paper torn by wind, streaming outwards, disintegrating. But the child stands there. The child does not move.

Some days later Tony and Mary eat their breakfast and leave the flat. As they walk through the door they stop.

'What are they?' he asks, but she doesn't know.

Round the door are lights, yellow, white, blue. Music plays, distant like music from across a park or over rooftops. They recognise the tune as their own.

The lights were shattered as the bullets hit them. Afterwards no broken bulbs could be found, but the smashed fragments of the tune littered the floor beside their bodies.

(h)

No one had ever felt this way before. They knew it. Only in fiction were there realistic parallels for what they felt. If they could have chosen how to die, they would have chosen to die as they did, in each other's arms.

After their death, the disaffected young took them to their hearts, sang their song, adopted their names. They lived again on teeshirts, banners, posters, slogans aerosolled on walls. Their love was absolute – conceived in ideological purity, forged in political action, destroyed by the forces of repression, made eternal by myth.

He was buried in England, she in Ireland. Her photograph was carried on her coffin in an image like that of Christ. At her graveside six black-hooded men fired pistol salutes.

His family took his body back. Some while later the grave was desecrated, and for ever afterwards a rumour circulated that his heart had been removed and buried beside her.

part two

Processions with banners scattered under the sharp crack of fire. Priests, crouched, with white handkerchiefs, led men carrying the wounded and dying. Girls were found lashed to lamp-posts, their hair shorn and their scalps glistening with black tar. Children hurled half-bricks, cobbles, petrol bombs, or played among derelict buildings and burned-out buses. Slogans glared from high walls. Prisoners starved themselves in cells daubed with their own shit. Bombs, grenades, mortars burst in shops, cars, garages, police stations, a bandstand. The streets are strewn with rubber bullets, broken glass, stones, wooden spars.

Cars are fired on at roadblocks. Kidnap victims lie on their beds at gunpoint. Bombs knock out windows in quiet streets. A teacher is shot in front of his class, a policeman killed on crossing-patrol, bodies lie under blankets in alleys, farmyards, roads.

A bomb in a London pub kills several soldiers, a handful of civilians, a Labrador dog.

Turn the page.

CESARE PAVESE

THE DEVIL IN THE HILLS

Cesare Pavese is now generally regarded as one of the most important writers of the century. This novel is among his best work. It is the story of a young married man, rich and self-indulgent, who has an elderly mistress, and whilst participating in the debauchery prevalent amongst his friends, nevertheless desires to lead a more useful life.

sceptre

BOMAN DESAI

THE MEMORY OF ELEPHANTS

'THE MEMORY OF ELEPHANTS is the story of Homi Seervai, a young Parsi scientist living in the US who invents a memory machine, gets trapped into it and plunges into the collective unconscious . . . Desai's device is clever; he uses it to advantage, turning Homi into a witness of historical events. In this way the reader is told of the descent of the Parsis of India from their Arab defeated ancestors, the rulers of the Persian Empire'

The Observer

'Homi's backgrounds, his family, and India come to life with great vividness and humour. Added to that are rewarding insights into the alien wisdom of exiles. The observations are acute; you sense a generosity of spirit in Desai's way of looking at the world and at people'

Yorkshire Post

'An accomplished first novel, an ingenious approach to the family saga form. The author has brought off exactly what he set out to do'

Janice Elliott in The Independent

sceptre

SAM NORTH

THE AUTOMATIC MAN

In a bare high-rise flat, fear holds a young man in its grip. Victim of a vicious assault, he records in diary form the aftermath of what he terms the Original Incident. Through his eyes the city beyond his front door comes alive with hidden terrors; objects, especially knives, acquire a deadly significance; he is conscious of acting and reacting to people like an automaton; his girlfriend, held at an emotional distance, walks out. Only when real danger threatens does he find the courage to confront it and realise that, at last, he has fear under control.

Original, blackly humorous and terrifyingly real, THE AUTOMATIC MAN draws an arresting portrait of a life scarred by violence and a world distorted by imagination.

'London's brooding underbelly has long provided the setting for contemporary explorations of urban paranoia, yet few have achieved the seductive menace of THE AUTOMATIC MAN . . . North skilfully shows how we construct the bars of our own imprisonment. This is what neurosis is like'
City Limits

'A striking début, sharply written and worrying'
D. J. Taylor in The Sunday Times

sceptre

Current and forthcoming titles from Sceptre

MELVYN BRAGG

THE CUMBRIAN TRILOGY
FOR WANT OF A NAIL
JOSH LAWTON
THE MAID OF BUTTERMERE

RONALD FRAME

PENELOPE'S HAT

MARK OLDHAM

NEW VALUES

WILLIAM McILVANNEY

WALKING WOUNDED

BOOKS OF DISTINCTION